THE GL

Set in Cork in the eal... humour and naked honesty, *The Glass Mountain* brilliantly encapsulates the world of college – the friendships and love affairs, summer jobs and shared flats. Maeve is nineteen and wants to be a punk, but she can't spit and doesn't understand anarchy. She tries to throw a brick through a window but almost brains herself in the process. She's doing science but can't stomach the smell of formaldehyde. She spends a lot of time eating chocolates, and drinking cider at Curtains Bar. But there are secrets at Curtains - secrets which involve Gret, Maeve's best friend; Fred, the post-grad student addicted to seances; and the glamorous Josie, who disintegrates into alcoholism and blames everyone else for her drinking. Secrets frighten Maeve, and so do power games, but by relating her fears to her beloved fairy tales and ghost stories, she learns how different people and families may give her some kind of guide for living.

MARTINA EVANS

Martina Evans was born in 1961 and grew up in County Cork. She trained as a radiographer at St Vincent's Hospital, Dublin and moved to London in 1988. She has also published a collection of poetry, *The Iniscarra Bar and Cycle Rest* and her second poetry collection *All Alcoholics are Charmers* was published in autumn 1998 by Anvil Press.

ALSO BY MARTINA EVANS

Midnight Feast

Martina Evans

THE GLASS MOUNTAIN

V

VINTAGE

Published by Vintage 1998

2 4 6 8 10 9 7 5 3 1

First published in Great Britain by
Sinclair-Stevenson in 1997

Vintage
Random House, 20 Vauxhall Bridge Road,
London SW1V 2SA

Random House Australia (Pty) Limited
20 Alfred Street, Milsons Point, Sydney
New South Wales 2061, Australia

Random House New Zealand Limited
18 Poland Road, Glenfield,Auckland 10,
New Zealand

Random House South Africa (Pty) Limited
Endulini, 5A Jubilee Road, Parktown 2193,
South Africa

Random House UK Limited Reg. No. 954009

A CIP catalogue record for this book
is available from the British Library

ISBN 0 09 927652 6

Papers used by Random House UK Ltd are natural,
recyclable products made from wood grown in sustain-
able forests. The manufacturing processes conform to the
environmental regulations of the country of origin

Printed and bound in Great Britain by
Cox & Wyman, Reading, Berkshire

For Declan

'How many roads must a man walk down before you can call him a man? The person who asked this question was good at asking questions. He was particularly interested in white doves and cannon balls, but his choicest question was as to how long a mountain can exist before it is washed out to sea.'

John Rety,
*Through the Anarchist Press:
a Column in Freedom*

Contents

Acknowledgements

Lyrics from the following songs are included with permission: 'Real Wild Child' (O'Keefe/Greenan/ Owens), copyright © 1958 MPL Comms., Inc. USA, Peermusic (UK) Ltd., 8–14 Verulam Street, London; 'Too Much Too Young' (Dammers), copyright © 1979 Plangent Visions Music Limited; 'Ghost Town' (Dammers), copyright © 1981 Plangent Visions Music Limited; 'Swords of a Thousand Men' (Tuderpole), copyright © 1981 Warner Bros Music Limited, Warner/Chappell Music Limited, London W1Y 3FA, reproduced by permission of International Music Publications Limited.

'A Great Hope Fell' by Emily Dickinson is reprinted by permission of the publishers and the Trustees of Amherst College from *The Poems of Emily Dickinson*, Thomas H. Johnson, ed., Cambridge, Mass.: The Belknap Press of Harvard University Press, Copyright © 1951, 1955, 1979, 1983 by the President and Fellows of Harvard College. The extract from *Wide Sargasso Sea* by Jean Rhys (Penguin Books, 1968), copyright © Jean Rhys, 1966, is reproduced by permission of Penguin Books Limited.

I would like to thank my editor Penny Hoare for her support.

PART ONE

· *Gazing Upwards* ·

· One ·

I thought that I was a punk until the night that the Beat and the Specials came to the Arc. Everyone came, even hippies humping along in their fawn afghan coats, biblical plaits swinging below their rainbow woven hats.

Queueing up with Ger was great, the gear knock. The sky was petrol blue, there was a fantastic smell of apples and alcohol from all the cider that was around the place and high above our heads three-foot high letters lit up crimson to say 'Arcadia Ballroom'. Just like hell.

Ger was a hippy and wore the worst clothes but I danced with her anyway because I was a tolerant punk. Besides, I admired her ambition. She wanted to be an English lecturer. I was sick in my stomach at the thought of having to work, having a job, having to listen to towering people telling me that I was useless.

When we got inside, Ger was dancing to the Clash, but it could have been Elton John for all she cared. She got out of breath quickly and leaned up against a pole, telling me about Fred's latest seance. 'The glass spelt out "Beelzebub" and the statue of Our Lady turned around three times on the mantelpiece!'

Fred was always having seances. It was very boring. I ran my fingers through my hair and tried to get another look around the hall.

'It's so bad you'd nearly believe him,' Ger said poking at a white stringy thing that was hanging out of the sleeve of her purple Indian dress. It looked too long for a handkerchief.

They were playing the Sex Pistols before the bands came on. 'Pretty Vacant'.

'Johnny Rotten is a genius,' I said.

'Is he?' said Ger and looked sick.

I'd mentioned Johnny Rotten to Ger before. His exciting thin body. His dangerous staring eyes. Ger asked me if he was like Byron and I said he was, not having a clue what Byron looked like. It was a disappointment to both of us when I showed Ger his picture. 'Jesus, he's like a mad weasel!' Ger shrieked.

'Ah, but look at his little furry torn jumper,' I said.

'Pull yourselves together.' Carl was ashamed of me. 'It was John Lydon who invented gobbing! Furry little jumpers, what kind of poxy language is that to be using about him!'

Spitting phlegm at people was called gobbing. It was a part of punk that I found hard to accept, so I tried to pretend that it wasn't happening, that it wasn't shooting past my face, that people weren't hawking all around me at every gig.

I was looking around for Carl and his friend Tom. Tom was a skinhead but he wore weird things like Farah trousers and coloured shirts with white peaky collars. His father's seventies clothes. They should have been desperate, but somehow, maybe because he was a skinhead, they looked unusual and interesting.

When we'd been waiting outside, I thought that I'd seen Carl swigging a bottle of cider at the end of the queue but I couldn't be sure. Just as I leaned forward to get a closer look, the queue moved. Turned an elbow into the Arc and I couldn't check any more.

Because Ger was a hippy she couldn't dance properly. Or didn't care. Her eyes were huge from magic mushrooms and her legs were bare under the long purple tassels of her dress. She never wore enough clothes. It used to make me shiver, but then I got used to it. Ger studied hard most of the week and took drugs at the weekend. She didn't have the time for a boyfriend. Her mother was a widow and she was afraid of losing the grant.

Not that my own money situation was too good. I didn't get any grant because my family hadn't passed the means test. My father was always going to politicians about it. *Where was it all going to end?* he kept asking. They were wiping the ground with the farmers.

I saw Fred. Fred worked in the physics department. I thought that he might have influence so I always said hello. Even though he was bad for my image. It was okay to hang around with Ger, that was kind of devil-may-care. But two hippies, well people would just think I was one too. *Show me your company and I'll tell you what you are,* my father was always saying.

'Was Ger telling you about our seance?'

'She said something about Beelzebub.'

I was sure that he was making it up. Fred lived with his older brother who was a GP in a big house on the Rochestown Road. Not the kind of house where you'd expect to find the light burning before the Sacred Heart. Maybe naked artistic sculptures or a few modern blobby paintings, but no holy statues.

A couple of punks went running up the hall past Fred. Their legs were thin and their boots were huge. They made deep hollow noises on the floorboards as they went past. They weren't from college. I knew by their hard faces.

I found it hard to take Fred seriously, his hair was so long and he was always touching my arm. But he had a first-class physics degree. I had to respect that, especially since I was having so much trouble passing those physics multiple-choice papers with the negative marking. I'd only managed to get above nought once.

'I'd believe you if you could prove to me that seances work.'

'We can do one at your place.'

I shivered when he said it, even though I thought seances were a load of rubbish.

There was a loud bash and with a start, I realized that the Beat were on. A wild drunken charge came from the bottom of the Arc. Skinheads dressed in black were everywhere, pogo dancing. Pushing each other and spitting at the band. Shouting out the words of 'Hands Off She's Mine'.

I stood and watched the Beat, trying to look normal even though I was on my own. Ger and Fred had gone into a corner to light up a joint. Avoiding scroungers. The hall got darker, smokier and the floor was hopping with the drumming of feet.

'Eeeh,' went a raucous voice into my ear and I jumped around.

Carl wore a black plastic raincoat. His face was like a sheet. He'd had his head just shaved and his red hair was glistening like crystallized ginger.

Everybody was pogoing. Carl caught my hand and we were jumping up and down too. I threw myself into it. 'Mirror in the Bathroom' came on. I had another quick look round as I was pogoing and I saw Tom talking to a crowd of skinheads. They were looking at me and Carl. I jumped higher. Carl squeezed my hand tightly, I could smell the cider on his breath. A woody smell like grass or pine needles.

'Eeeh, Carlo! On the ball, boy!'

I stopped jumping with a jolt and put my hand to my warm wet forehead. A cold dredge was lowered in my stomach. The Beat went off the stage and groups gathered, waiting for the Specials. I walked quickly towards Fred and Ger who were sitting on the ground, resting their backs against the wall.

Carl followed me. 'Maeve, don't be so sensitive! They're all pissed.'

'I don't care!'

'Eeeh, Carlo, boy!' The crowd of skinheads cheered again and whistled. I gave Carl a vicious look.

'Maeve, ignore them!'

'I can't!'

'Where's your fucking sense of humour?'

The crowd was growing restless, waiting for the Specials. A fight broke out at the back of the hall. Fred's eyes remained shut, his head flopped back against the wall.

I turned around. 'Carl Toner, who the fuck do you think you are?' I could see Tom laughing in the background.

Carl didn't say a word, he poked irritably with his boot at an uneven floorboard. Quick as anything I felt guilty.

'Can we talk upstairs?' I pointed to the gallery and then had another thought. 'I'm sorry, I forgot about the Specials. We'd better stay here.'

But Carl thought it was a good idea. 'We'll have an even better view up there.' He shouted at Tom: 'Have you got the Bulmer's?'

Tom came over, watching the bouncers carefully. He

took a flagon of cider out of his military-green coat and Carl grabbed it quickly.

'Come on,' Carl called, as he shoved the bottle into his pocket.

'Here's your hat, Carl,' another of the skinheads shouted, throwing him an old monkey hat. Carl put it on his head and the cheers grew again as we went up the stairs. Other groups joined in. A tall stringy fellow with green and pink hair was shouting, 'Go for it, ya langers!'

I decided to ignore them, this time. I told myself that it wasn't Carl's fault. But it was embarrassing and I was afraid that I would stumble on the stairs.

'How deep is your throat?' I could hear Tom singing.

When we got to the top, it seemed to be nothing but couples, clinging to each other. Like the back row of the cinema. One fellow had his hand down the front of a girl's blouse while she smoked a joint, giggling softly. Too late, I realized that the place was all wrong.

I jumped when someone groaned about two inches from my ankles. If only I could make an excuse, pretend to go to the loo and disappear. Taking in a deep breath I sat down in the space between two sprawling couples.

Carl strained as he tried to open the bottle. His wrists grew red under his frayed cuffs. I noticed with a twinge his long white fingers. His freckles, the size of flying saucers.

I took out a packet of cigarettes and offered him one. Carl shook his head. He didn't smoke. I hoped that he didn't think I smelt horrible. And I'd no sooner begun to worry about the smell of cigarettes when a huge curtain of cigarette smoke seemed to shake itself out around me. I was conscious of it every time I spoke or moved.

Carl moved closer and passed me the bottle. I shrank back into my shroud of smoke, arranged my mouth self-consciously into the smallest opening. The cider went down the wrong way. I starting gagging and coughing. I felt stupid, tears flowing out of my eyes and all the couples sitting up, suddenly. Staring. Carl banging my back. My big red face.

'Have some more quickly.' Carl urgently offered me the bottle when I'd stopped coughing. Like falling off a horse, you had to get back on the cider immediately.

I took a big slug and decided to say my bit as quick as I could. 'Carl . . .' Carl's white hand was right next to my leg. The flying saucers began to blur.

The pall of smoke stirred and drifted, it couldn't settle its borders. 'Carl, I think you're a great friend.' I stared at the way his white scalp shone very white between the red bristles on his head, 'And can't we just stay like that?'

It was bad enough saying something that bad. But then having to look at Carl's face looking at me.

I forgot what I was going to say next. I stared at this fellow sprawled across from us. Gnawing the neck off his girlfriend.

Carl smiled. 'Jesus, you had me worried coming up here. I thought I was about to be raped.' His lips had almost completely disappeared.

'Don't make fun of me, please. I'm sorry, honestly I am. Can't we pretend nothing happened?'

'Did something happen? I didn't notice.' Carl took another swig of cider. 'Actually, I will have one of your cigarettes.' I held out the packet and lit his cigarette.

We finished the packet in silence, cloaked in smoke, dancing dejectedly among the writhing couples in the gallery . . . *Much, much too young, now you're married with a kid when you should be having fun with me.*

The cider was warm and flat. Carl was rippling his pared lips in a very tough looking way. We swung our arms like mad. Ska dancing. *You've done too much, much too young . . . married with a son, when you should be having fun with me . . . chained to the cooker making currant buns for tea.*

We heard shouts and whistles. Tom was jumping up and down. Waving at Carl from below. *I'd love to spread manure in your bed of roses.*

'We might as well go down,' Carl said carelessly. 'It's nearly time to go.'

Ain't you heard of the starving millions. Ain't you heard of contraception. We went down the wooden staircase. Carl stuffed the empty cider bottle in the pocket of his white raincoat. *Try wearing a cap.*

Carl said something but I couldn't hear. It seemed important. Somebody screamed from the bottom of the hall, and a crowd of girls danced right up against us. I avoided them, afraid of the cigarettes they were waving in their hands.

The skinheads had joined Ger and Fred. They were teasing Ger. I could see by the way she was flicking her hair.

'Was he any good?' Tom asked me.

The band were playing their last song and everyone was pogoing. I had to jump up and down like mad. Even though I didn't want to. Not one bit.

The hall grew bright later and I went with Ger to queue up for the coats. Ger got sick in the corner.

'Sorry, I couldn't help it. It just happened really quickly.'

'You should try and stay off the magic mushrooms.'

'It's not the mushrooms!' Ger said and wiped her

face with the piece of white cheesecloth. It looked like the sleeve of a blouse.

Carl had gone with Tom and he hadn't bothered to say goodbye properly. It was cold on McCurtain Street. I shivered inside my donkey jacket. A real authentic donkey jacket from a London building site. Carl had sold it to me for a fiver, even though he could have got a lot more for it. He had been to London the summer of eighty and had seen all the great bands, stood next to Joe Jackson in a club and asked the Bodysnatchers for a light.

Ger's face and hands were blue, her nineteen-forties coat was threadbare. 'So what will you do?' I asked, as we walked down Patrick Street.

'I think I'll come to London with you,' Ger said casually.

· *Two* ·

As we walked down the street, Ger asked me did I know that I'd been in the 'undressed' circle with Carl. I remembered all those moaning couples, how I'd walked through. Stiff and red-faced. I went red again.

The last people I wanted to meet then were Carl and Tom who sprang out of the shadows with Best. Tom and Best had shaving foam all over their hands and I think that they wanted to chase us. Ger just told them to piss off. I noticed how Tom obeyed Ger.

'You look a bit pale,' he said and fell into step with Ger. I followed silently behind with Carl. Best ran ahead leaping and shouting to himself. He'd let his fringe grow long out of his shaved head and he'd dyed it gold. He looked like a bumblebee with his eyes bulging below the black and gold.

Tom was talking like mad to Ger. I could see him sneaking looks at her pink knees every time the wind whipped at her skirt.

'You're kind to old men,' I heard him saying.

'Am I?'

'You're very nice to Pierce.'

'Am I?' repeated Ger, cool as anything.

Pierce owned Curtains Bar and he loaned Ger books

and gave us free drink when he thought that no one was looking. I thought that Pierce and his wife Myra dressed very ordinary, but Carl insisted that they were old hippies. Told me that I had to be careful, the slightest encouragement and they'd be singing 'Joe Hill'.

'I have to go up to see the nuns at the Sacred Heart tomorrow,' Tom said. Another quick look at Ger's knees. I stopped humming. Ger must have noticed him looking because she began to button up the end of her coat.

'Do you?' Ger said. There was a genuine note of interest in her voice now. She liked anything a bit unusual.

'Sister Eucharia's my mother's cousin. The old lady's been on to me for ages to visit her.'

'Who's the old lady?'

'My mother.' I saw Tom's mother in a flash. A tiny white-haired lady.

'She hates going up there, so I said that I'd go up there instead.'

'Aren't you very good.' Ger was only half teasing.

'Oh, I like my mother. I don't mind doing things for her.' Tom lowered his voice and I tried to get closer to them. Carl was breathing loudly through his mouth. Could he be doing it deliberately to drown out their voices?

'It's very dark,' I said, trying to pretend that my ears weren't hanging off with the strain.

'What's she like?' Ger was getting more interested.

'She's young-looking with long hair. A bit like yours, long and black.'

'She doesn't sound like an old lady!'

'Ah she's good crack.'

'That's good.' Ger sounded strange and thoughtful. 'What does she teach?'

'French. We go to France every year on our holidays.'

Ger went quiet then. I knew she didn't like talking about holidays. Her mother was a widow and a dressmaker. She hadn't a bob. They never went anywhere. My family never went on holidays either. Not because we didn't have money, but because my father was narrow-minded and mean. *'Twas far from holidays you were reared!*

I looked at Carl guiltily. His arms were very long hanging out of his black raincoat. Yet he didn't seem that forlorn. I got the impression he was laughing at me listening to the others.

Tom's yellow Volkswagon was parked halfway up Patrick's Hill. Patrick's Hill was as steep as the side of a mountain and Collin's Barracks was right on top. Coming down the other side was Richmond Hill and that was even worse. I nearly went flying up there one night coming out of a party. Of course everyone said that I was flaming.

I held my breath when Tom left off the handbrake and the car shot down to the traffic lights. Carl pointed out the sweep of lights along Patrick Street. I nodded feebly, feeling like my mother. The way she clung on to the hanging strap every time my father overtook a tractor.

It was quiet in the car. Tom's tape machine was broken, after chewing up two tapes of the Cure and the three compilation tapes Carl had recorded of all his Two Tone singles. Best was sitting in the corner, reading *Hot Press*, his body jerking like a lifeless puppet to the sudden stops and starts of the car.

I went red again remembering the 'undressed'

circle. Carl didn't even try to speak to me. Ger was holding in the nausea; I knew by the way that she was sitting.

I opened my rucksack. The smell of chocolate and lead pencils was so beautiful I caught my breath. I always carried a load of chocolate and pencils which I kept sharpening. Sharp as stilettos. I bought them in art shops. '*Staedtler* Tradition HB', with the red and thin black stripes, the white stripe encircling the top. So elegant.

Whenever I passed a sweet-shop, I bought something, so I hardly ever ran out. I liked small things. Chocolate saws and hammers, white chocolate mice, Kalypso bars, chocolates that came in little coloured foil cases, called ices. Ices were rare, only a few shops sold them, so I bought a good few whenever I found them.

I opened a bag of Maltesers and offered Carl one. He shook his head. I could still hear his breathing. Stertorous. That was a scientific word. I wondered if my scientific days weren't over.

Then Tom said he was nearly out of petrol and had anyone a fiver. Best spent ages fishing in his army trousers and came up with one-fifty. Carl had two pounds. Tom had nothing, Ger was too sick to speak and I kept eating my Maltesers.

Carl was annoyed. 'That two pounds was for the film club!'

Carl went to the film club every Friday night. That's where I met him first. He'd been sitting at the back, with his legs stretched out in front of him, relaxing, and I came in late and fell over his feet. When I got talking to him he said that the music from *The Third Man* was his favourite film music too. I hummed a bit

15

of it for him when we were walking home and he said that I hadn't a note in my head.

I dived into my rucksack quickly. 'Carl, I've loads. Look here's one-fifty.'

But Carl wouldn't take it. He said that he'd changed his mind about going to the film club. My heart gave an awful lurch when he said it and I tried to push the money into his hands.

His hands felt cold, he pulled them away and folded his arms.

'Hang on to your money, Maeve,' he said in a terrible kind voice as if I was some unfortunate creature he had to take pity on.

Tom drove up to the petrol pumps really fast. He nearly knocked down the petrol-pump attendant.

'Go easy.'

'The fucker came out of nowhere, for god's sake look at him. The Ku Klux Klan.'

The petrol-pump attendant was tiny, wearing a cream-coloured duffle coat with the hood up. A couple of bright red spikes peeped out of the hood. He looked frozen.

'How much?'

'Three-fifty.'

'Three-fifty what?' snapped the small thin face in the cream-coloured hood.

'Three pounds fifty, you langer.'

'Three pounds fifty what?' the pinched lips snapped again.

'Jesus Christ! It's all I've got!'

'*Please*, say *please*,' Best whispered. 'That's Jimmy Barry. He's fucking dangerous.'

'Oh, now I see,' Tom roared. 'Three pounds fifty *please*.'

'Don't mention it, boy,' Jimmy Barry said. He went around to the petrol tank, smiling sourly.

I went to get some Fox's Fruits from the shop at the service station.

Walking across the tarmac, I heard this angry voice. 'What in the fuck are you?'

I looked at Jimmy Barry, surprised. 'I'm a punkette,' I said.

'You are like fuck.'

'Shut up!' I said, mad.

'Sure there's no such thing as a punkette. You can't gob and you'd be no good in a fight.'

'Of course I would.'

'Yerra go 'way and don't be annoying me. With your country accent. I betcha anything you can't gob.'

I stood there, mad and mortified. I was going to try and spit at him when Tom rolled down the window and shouted out to know what was going on.

'Fuck off,' I said to Jimmy Barry, feeling a bit better when I saw Tom.

Jimmy Barry only laughed. 'What size are your feet? They must be about three. Jesus, they look fierce stunted.'

'Size five. Fuck off!' I said again and began to run towards the shop.

'Middle-class fucking eedjit. What punk in their right mind would be seen at a Two Tone concert?' he roared after me.

I stood at the grill composing myself and trying to remember what it was that Tom wanted. I wondered where Jimmy Barry got to know about things like middle class. *'Twas far from middle class you were reared!*

I turned around when I heard the shouts. Best, Carl and Tom had got out of the car, I could see them arguing with Jimmy Barry and I tried to rush over to stop them. I dropped my Fox's Fruits on the way and had to run back to pick them up.

Ger had got out of the car and was getting sick into a flower bed with an Esso sign in the middle of it.

'College fucking crowd, ye make me sick. Pretending to be punks for a few years until ye're accountants.'

Accountants was the worst possible thing he could have called us. Best threw his *Hot Press* to one side and went for Jimmy's throat.

'Get away, ya langer.' Jimmy Barry lashed out and the hood of his duffle fell back showing his head covered in bright red spikes. He turned the petrol on Best, spraying it right into his eyes. Best fell back and stood in a ball with his fists over his face.

Ger finished getting sick, wiped her face with the piece of cheesecloth again and threw it in the bin.

'Come away from that fool,' she said and helped Best to a water tap that was at the back of the station. I followed. Best was screaming and Ger held his eyelids open while I splashed water at them. Best was a useless patient. He kept trying to close his eyes and accusing Ger of digging her nails into him on purpose. The smell of petrol was vicious. Ger looked flushed and invigorated after emptying her stomach. 'You have to suffer now, the petrol was your nemesis,' she told Best. 'Go on, Maeve! Give him plenty water. Wash out his eyes completely.'

When we led Best back round to the car, Tom had blood dripping down his nose. 'That's fucking out of order!' Tom held a big wad of tissues against his nose. They looked like my tissues and I was going to say who opened my rucksack except I didn't want to sound petty.

'Anyone else for a bit of petrol?' Jimmy Barry asked.

Carl was raging, he kept making dashes and Jimmy Barry kept fending him off with little squirts. Carl had two funny lumps on either side of his face where he was chewing the insides of his cheeks. 'You could have blinded him,' he yelled.

'I'll get you yet, you fucker.' Best kept giving painful looks from between his fingers.

'I'm reporting you to your manager,' Tom said and jumped back when Jimmy Barry squirted another bit of petrol at him.

'Where's your anarchy now?' Jimmy Barry shouted and turned the petrol on full again.

We all ran back into the car and Tom started the engine up straight away. 'He's fucking mad!' he said and spun the car out of the yard.

Best had taken his hands off his eyes now, they were red and weeping. The car stank of petrol. 'Don't anyone light a cigarette!' screamed Tom.

'Why was he going on about anarchy?' I asked Carl.

'Because punks are supposed to support anarchy. That's why it's stupid college students trying to be punks.'

'Why?' I said, wishing I knew exactly what anarchy was.

'Because college students are just conforming to society by getting degrees which will lead to jobs within the status quo.'

'Oh,' I said.

He leaned back in the seat and looked at me sympathetically. 'What was he saying to you anyway?'

'He was saying that I couldn't be a punk because I was a woman. He called me a culchie and he said that I couldn't even spit.'

'Well it's true.' Best gave me a bleary eye.

'Bloody bastard!' Tom shouted. 'What did he go picking on you for!'

'He said that I was a middle-class eedjit and that my feet were stunted!'

There was a choking sound from Best. He exploded into horrible laughter.

'In all fairness,' Tom said, 'it's the lowest of the low picking on Maeve.'

As if I was a complete headcase, only fit for pity.

Tom suddenly stopped the car on the middle of the Wilton Road and wheeled around. 'What are you going to do?' Ger screamed. 'Can't you leave it alone!'

'No, he needs to be taught a lesson.' Tom was grim, racing up the gears.

'I can't fight in this condition,' Best said as the car pulled up at the petrol pumps again.

'I'm not asking you to fight,' Tom said and rolled down the window.

Jimmy Barry stood there with a taunting smirk on his lemon face. 'D'ya forget something?'

'No.' Tom rolled down the window. 'You sexist bastard! I'll be down in the morning to the Guards in the Bridewell.'

'You will in your fucking hole!' Jimmy Barry said and flashed a knife. Tom didn't have time to roll up the window. He swerved out of the yard quickly. Looking back, I could see Jimmy Barry's lips forming the words, 'Langer Dan.'

'Oh, you really sorted him out,' Ger said in a sarcastic voice. She had to get sick again before we reached home. When she got out of the car, Carl leaned over to whisper in my ear. But he was only saying that he would take that one-fifty off me after all.

'Middle-class eedjit!' Carl muttered to himself for no reason.

'I'm not middle class!'

'What are you?'

'I don't know. I don't know why everyone is talking about middle class all of a sudden. Nobody speaks about it at home.'

'What do they speak about?'

'Well you're either a small farmer or a big farmer or a teacher or a publican or you live in a cottage.'

'What are you?'

'We did have a biggish farm, but my father sold off a load of land to a builder.'

'Oh well, if he's got a load of money you're middle class.'

'He says he's broke and we only have a small farm now.'

'Then you must be lower-middle class!'

'Jesus, that's the pits altogether.'

'Lower-middle class is definitely the poxiest.' Carl folded his arms and said, 'Of course now that I know you're only lower-middle class, I'll be changing my attitude.'

'How do you mean?' I burst out, suddenly terrified at the thought that I might be vile lower-middle class. 'My father's got a workman on the farm, my grand-uncle was the Lord Abbot of Glenstall Abbey and my father's got twenty-five first cousins priests.'

'Twenty-five?'

Carl kept whistling and I was afraid he'd tell the others, so I asked him straight away, 'What does your father do?' Carl gave a quick look at Ger. She was leaning her head against the window and she had her eyes closed.

'Swear you won't say anything.'

'I swear.' My heart beat faster. Carl's face was so near. All red and gold and white.

'He's an accountant.'

· *Three* ·

Tuesday night I stood outside the film club. Everyone else had filed in through the thick wooden doors. There was silence inside except for the sound of music. The film had started, but Carl hadn't come. I took a mint out of the pocket of my donkey jacket and crunched it heartlessly. The splinters shot up between my teeth. I never cared much about my teeth. I cared even less now.

Carl had said the previous Friday that he was definitely coming, that he *had* to see *Apocalypse Now*. But that was before the night at the Arc. He was probably sick of me. Or showing me that I wasn't that important.

And what about the one-fifty I'd loaned him?

Everyone was staring when I peered around the seats in the film club hoping that he was hidden somewhere, tying his shoelace or adjusting the elastoplast that he wore over the tear in his Doc Martens.

They all knew that I was looking for Carl and they probably all knew that he was sick of me too. I wondered how many of those confident sprawling couples from the Arc were posted around the room.

I peeled the gold wrapper off the top of a packet of Rolos and put the chocolate on my tongue to dissolve.

It didn't help though. It made me feel strange and queasy.

I wished that Ger was around. I wanted to talk to her, to tell her how I was going to treat Carl with a distant unapproachable kindness, so poignant that it would make him grind his teeth with agony at the loss of my friendship.

I missed Ger. The smell of the musk she wore from that grey shiny bottle. Made by Alyssa Ashley, two pounds ninety-nine pence in Roches Stores. I'd bought her the biggest bottle for her birthday and it was still only two pounds and ninety-nine pence. Enough musk to last her until she was twenty-five. She'd have her Masters by then, she said.

I went down the dark stairs, through the wooden doors and came out into the dimly lit campus. I shuddered passing the medical-school building, where they fought over the best legs to dissect and threw garlands of intestines around each other's necks saying 'Halloha'. A medical student called John told me all this at a disco. He said the walls were lined with jars of foetuses and then congratulated me for not blushing when he said the word 'foetus'.

He seemed to smell of formaldehyde. I couldn't figure out if it was really him or my imagination, but it got stronger when he moved nearer. He was with this other medical student called Claire. She'd moved from New York when she was about ten, but she still looked like an American. She didn't have an American accent, except now and then she said 'I guess'. She had a tan and blonde hair like one of Charlie's Angels. Nobody believed that she was doing med. She was too good-looking and glamorous. They assumed that she was doing arts. John didn't believe that I was doing

24

science either. Not because I was so glamorous but because he said that I looked half mad.

'What did you do that to your hair for? It's not a bit feminine.'

'Oh, do you think I should perm it?' I asked him, really sarcastic.

'I don't like perms.' John sounded puzzled and thoughtful. 'They're so unnatural.'

Carl and Ger were the only people who copped when I was being sarcastic.

'You stink of formaldehyde!' I said to him, furious to think that he thought I'd ask him for advice about my hair.

I was haunted by the smell of formaldehyde. Zoology had been a lovely subject at school, with lots of intricate diagrams to colour in with my colouring pencils, and interesting Latin words. Sister Joseph's wide wooden table was clean and dry, stacked with pictures of brains and hearts. Notes on the reproductive system were handed out silently and tactfully. We hadn't dissected as much as a ladybird.

When I arrived at my first zoology practical, we were all given a dissecting kit. Khaki-coloured and lined with tiny pockets, filled with scalpels and tweezer-type things. Made me think of archaeologists, colonial types with knee-high socks, King Solomon's Mines.

My first zoology practical was where I met Claire. She was sitting next to me wearing a pale blue fluffy jumper inside her American soft denim dungarees. She was friendly, opening up a new packet of scalpel blades and giving me a shiny one to replace the blunt yellow blade that seemed to be rusting onto the end of my scalpel.

Rows of carcasses lay along the tables. Everyone had

a rabbit in front of them. I looked down at the grey, hairless, rubbery thing. The skin had a purple sheen and was almost transparent, veins showing up like rivers on a satellite map.

A tall man with a beard gave instructions at the top of the class. His face was square and unemotional. We would dissect the rabbit over the next four weeks, starting with the central nervous system. Then we would begin on the dogfish.

'Fair enough,' said a tall black-haired fellow with glasses.

I looked at him and Claire started laughing.

'I can't wait to get stuck in,' he explained, noticing Claire who was starting to choke. 'My name is Dom,' he said in a desperate attempt to arrest Claire's laughter.

But Claire only waved her hand at him apologetically. 'You've started me off!'

Claire was always giggling. And it wasn't just delicate titters. It was snorts and throwing her body around when it got too much. The zoology demonstrator kept checking his flies every time she broke out.

The blade of Dom's scalpel was old and blunt. It baulked on the elastic skin of the rabbit. Claire gave him a new blade and cut her rabbit easily, heaving every now and then with a left-over giggle. I asked her had she done any dissection before. She said that she'd seen her teacher do a frog once at her school.

I tried the first cut and even with my new blade made a jagged tear along the rabbit. The smell of formaldehyde rose and sickened me. I could feel the fumes at the back of my throat, a thickness I couldn't swallow. I jabbed at the rabbit feebly with my knife.

'You better get stuck into it.' Dom leaned over paternally. 'Keep your eye on the clock.' He nodded in the direction of the huge white dial that was suspended over the demonstrator's desk. A red second hand swept around but it was only half past two.

'I wish it was five o'clock and I could get out!'

Dom gave me a look of consternation and bent his bony shoulders over his rabbit.

'The smell is awful,' Claire admitted, but she went on cutting and even though she was unsure and made mistakes, she was able to extract the fine nerves of the rabbit and uncover the nervous system.

Dom was really brilliant. I asked him if he was going to be a surgeon.

'I'm only doing science,' he said. 'I'm hoping to get teaching.'

I couldn't bear to touch the rabbit. I wrapped a cloth around my hand and hacked half-heartedly. I tried to peel out the nerves, but they came out broken and maimed, chunks of flesh hanging onto them.

Claire got the brain out. It was yellow and shrivelled, the right and the left side clearly divided by an indented line. Claire giggled, holding it in her hand. 'I'm going to put it in my brother's dinner tonight.'

She took a tissue out of her pocket and wrapped the brain up. 'I can't wait to see his face.'

Claire said she was getting used to the smell of the formaldehyde, but I thought that it was getting worse. I managed to get the brain out of my rabbit, even though the left and the right side were nearly torn apart. Half-dissected torn nerves lay abandoned around my rabbit. The demonstrator toured the benches. He lifted his eyebrows when he passed my section.

At half past five, we left the building. It was dark already and I half staggered in the wind that threw itself at us, heavy as a winter overcoat. The orange street-lamps and the darkness made me feel strange. Unreal. As if big brown tables and rabbit's insides were homely things and the city was a stranger.

I got the flu and missed the next three zoology practicals.

By the time I recovered and plucked up the courage to return, the dogfish had arrived. This time I didn't even try to dissect the greenish stiff carcass that the demonstrator had taken out of a box full of pointing jaws. I left the room with my handkerchief over my mouth.

It was easy for Carl to tell me to go back. *He* was doing psychology. A nice safe subject on paper. Nothing real.

What about my one-fifty? He could have at least come to give me my money even if he didn't want to see me.

Science had changed so much between school and university. Even chemistry seemed far away now. A bald whispery man gave lectures, pronouncing the word 'water' like an Englishman.

I shivered in the dark thinking about the chemistry labs. I had to use bunsen burners and volatile liquids. No one cared if I blew myself up. They went on demonstrating through the winter afternoons, their distant voices bored and monotonous. Outside the windows grew dark and menacing, as if time was running out. As if volatile liquids would soon finish us all off.

I used to know lots of things about science at school. Now I knew nothing. Lecturers kept talking about how theories of physics were changing. As if this was exciting. As if I wanted to kill myself learning some theory that wouldn't be true next week.

28

I wanted to give it up and do arts. But I couldn't say that to my father. He'd say that I was going to break him. He'd walk around the farmyard with his tongue hanging out, sticking pitchforks into plastic bags. Saying that the sheriff was going to come one of these weeks and we'd all be out on the side of the road. *While you're up at the uni plastering muck all over your eyes. When will I see the return of my money?* Sometimes he'd throw down the pitchfork and start throwing buckets of water around the yard. By the way cleaning.

The only time I ever mentioned doing arts, he asked me if I wanted him to end up in Queer Street.

· *Four* ·

It seemed an alright thing to do. To order a pint of Bulmers. But I didn't feel alright or comfortable, rocking on top of a high bar-stool. I could see my face in the mirror, looking frantic between a bottle of Jameson and Bols cherry brandy.

We always drank in Curtains. It had a brilliant jukebox. They had the Jam, the Beat, the Specials and the Cure. They also had a few old sixties songs, like 'A Whiter Shade of Pale' and some Moody Blues stuff. Sops for the hippies, Carl called them.

I secretly liked the sops for hippies. I would throw my eyes up when some old thirty-year-old put them on, but a few times I began to sway in spite of myself. Just as well Carl thought that I was taking the piss.

I didn't have the same interest in the bands now that I wasn't really a punk. If I wasn't sure of something then I gave it up. I wasn't proud of this trait, but it was easy for me to feel hopeless. I was the same with science. If I couldn't get some of it right, I gave up on the whole thing. Failed scientist. Failed punk. *I know by your face you're going to fail,* my father said every time I went home. Fixing my fate.

I still had to wear my punk clothes though. I didn't have any others. And I still wore the make-up because

I looked like a pig without it. Small pale eyes. Ugh! I looked in between the Jameson and the cherry brandy, nervously checking that my eyes were well ringed with black.

Pierce and Myra Curtain were nice to students, but you had to be careful that they didn't start on about their own student days. Drawing comparisons between them and us.

Myra was on her own this evening, fussing with the cash register, unloading bags of coppers into the tuppenny and penny compartments. She wore an off-white full-length coat and strands of her untidy ponytail were scattered over the navy and green scarf she wore knotted around her neck.

'Hoping to bump into someone, are you?' Myra said, noisily chucking the tuppenny pieces.

'I'm thirsty, actually,' I said, red at the thought that someone might think I was desperate for company. Maybe even think that I was looking for Carl.

'I'll get your cider for you, now,' Myra said, but still kept on chucking the coins.

I wished that she'd hurry up. Without a drink, my hands felt heavy and awkward. I put them on the counter and tapped.

'I'm coming, I said.' Myra sounded annoyed.

'Oh, I didn't mean it,' I replied, but I couldn't explain that I was only trying to occupy my hands. I slung my hands off the counter and they hung down the sides of the stool. Too long.

Myra filled the pint and set it down in front of me. 'Will you be able for that now?'

'How come you never ask Ger that?'

'Yeah, but she drinks it all the time. The most you ever drink in a night is two bottles of Stag.'

I looked at my surreal reflection again. 'I'm going to drink it, slowly.'

'You're right, too,' Myra said and lifted out a huge cardboard box of new whiskey glasses. She took a glass-cloth and began to polish the dust off them.

Carl's angry face came back to me. I tried to think of something else, but there was nothing except painful thoughts. The brightly lit windows of the science laboratories. All those other students who were writing down results and equations, and slicing thin slivers of green botany stuff to look at under their microscopes. Comparing results. Loaning each other things.

'When I think of myself here with Pierce. Tied down for the rest of my days.' Myra moved the whiskey bottles to make more mirror space. 'When I think of myself, stuck here. A young woman!' Myra took the elastic band off her ponytail and shook her hair out. 'A young woman!' she repeated and stared in between the whiskey bottles with a wondering look.

I looked at our faces in the glass. They looked just as mad as each other. And Myra wasn't a young woman! Carl said that she'd told him one night that she was thirty-eight. There were loads of grey wisps in her hair.

'Your hair is nice down,' I said, quickly, hoping that the horror hadn't shown on my face.

'Don't be silly, I'm like a witch.'

'You're not!' I protested a bit much. 'You look beautiful, like Lady Macbeth.'

'Well, thank *you*.' Myra didn't sound pleased.

'No, I mean it, there was a really brilliant Lady Macbeth at the opera house a few years ago. I forget her name.'

Lady Macbeth seemed to have shocked Myra back into normality, because she gathered her hair back into the elastic band and took the wild look out of her eyes. She opened the cash register. 'Here's ten pence. Go and put on a song to cheer us up.'

How did she know I was sad? I thought that my eyes had a hard set when I looked in the mirror. I'd been practising it.

'And for god's sake none of that awful punk stuff. Put on Billy Jo Spears or whatever you like apart from punk,' Myra added. 'We don't have to pretend now we're on our own.'

Billy Jo Spears was one of my secret favourites. I pressed 14A for 'Blanket On the Ground' and went back to my stool quickly before the song started. The *dwong dwong* of country and western guitar began, I felt it go bump bump just under my ribcage and then the bar door opened. I held my breath as a figure in a raincoat stopped on the threshold. It was Carl. Wiping rain from his streaming face.

'Carl Toner!' Myra exclaimed. 'Here's your friend, Maeve, she's been waiting for you all evening.'

'I wasn't,' I said, frantically, trying to shout over Billy Jo Spears. Myra had just turned the volume right up. She was tapping in time along the Guinness and Murphy dispensers.

'Maeve's choice,' Myra said, nodding at the jukebox.

I got down off the stool despairingly and went over to Carl. He turned to look at me but before I could say a word, the door opened again. Tom came in with Ger. 'Blanket On the Ground' got louder and louder. Myra kept turning up the volume.

Tom and Carl started laughing, but they didn't make any sarky comments to Myra. Myra lit a cigarette and started moving seductively up and down the bar singing. I noticed Carl and Tom looking at her admiringly. She looked kind of fine in her way. Maybe if you were a man you'd probably think that she'd give you wild experiences.

I wouldn't have minded it too much if Carl had spoken to me, but he just kept staring at Myra.

'Sit down with me.' I dragged Ger to a table in the corner. 'You've no idea what I've been through.'

'What's wrong?'

'It's Myra. She was acting weird.'

'Did she take down her hair and say that she was a young woman?'

'How did you know?'

'She did the same to me last Thursday afternoon. I came in to go to the loo and when I came out she was ranting and raving in front of the mirror.'

'Bloody hell.' I bit into my finger.

Carl was at the jukebox with Tom. I could hear bits of their conversation. I remembered my one-fifty again. What had he done with it?

'Put on "A Whiter Shade of Pale" for a laugh,' Tom said. Carl punched the keys with his freckled fingers. They probably knew that I liked that one too.

'Have you worked out what you're going to do?' I asked Ger listlessly, turning my back to the jukebox.

'I've told you already that I'm going to England. You know that. Why do you keep asking me?'

'Oh yes, I forgot.'

'I'll never understand you. You've been begging me to come for the last three months.'

Begging? Did I beg?

Myra had taken her coat off and was giving directions. 'Go straight on until you come to a T-junction, turn right, then the road goes on for a while, veer left when you come to a V.'

I felt a sudden dislike for Myra. What if she had made me put 'Blanket On the Ground' on the jukebox

34

just to discredit me in the eyes of Carl? And now she was hogging Tom and Carl, giving those stupid directions just to show off the sleeves of her stupid batwing jumper. Maybe Carl thought that batwing sleeves were quaint. Maybe Carl liked thirty-eight-year-old women with wisps of grey in their hair.

I turned back to Ger. There were black streaks all over her face, tears coming out of her eyes.

Ger was always as cool as anything. I'd never seen her cry before.

I panicked a bit. 'Stop, Ger,' I said, really stupid.

Ger's tears kept flowing. I didn't know what to do. It felt like someone had got a heart attack or a stroke and I had to do artificial resuscitation.

I pulled myself together. 'Go to the loo and I'll follow you.' I pushed Ger and she went slowly, her thin coat hanging limply from her back like some kind of protest.

I glanced quickly at Carl and Tom, but they weren't looking. Myra seemed to be still giving directions, ' . . . third exit on the roundabout and go along a narrow windy road until you can go no further . . .' I wondered if I should get a black jumper like Myra's. Maybe if I wore it with Docs, it would look kind of cool.

Ger was standing against the wall, crying with her mouth open and no sound coming out. I wanted to put my arms around her, but I couldn't. Partly because she was so reserved, but also because I wasn't very demonstrative myself.

My father was a lunatic. You'd never kiss him and my mother she wasn't much good either. She never had any time for embraces. She spent her whole time obsessed with my father and what she called his rude health. She was always commenting on how fresh and unwrinkled his skin was, how he'd the face of a man twenty years younger, how he was going to drive her into an early grave with his tempers. And he said that his heart could go at any minute and look at the ulcer on his leg and then he'd roll up his trousers and she'd pull up her skirt and they'd compare their varicose veins. They did not go in for embracing.

Ger's musk got stronger as she cried. No matter how often I asked her she wouldn't tell what was wrong. Finally she told me that she was worried about the exams.

I laughed. 'God, your only problem is whether you'll get Honours or not.'

'And what's wrong with wanting to get Honours?' Ger demanded snuffily, waves of warm musk drifting from the folds of her clothes every time she wiped at her eyes.

I was hoping to just pass, but I had to understand it was different for Ger and I went on a bit too quickly about how I never knew anyone who read or knew as much. If she didn't get Honours the Dean should be shot. I should have known that there was more to it than that but I was in too much of a rush to get out before Carl left. As I pulled Ger back to the bar, I'd no respect for myself. I knew I was selfish.

· *Five* ·

I had a pain in my stomach. Thinking about Carl. I
went to May's. May's was a tiny sweet-shop down at
the back of the courthouse. She'd just got a new box
of chocolate ices. May was shy and always chewing.
She blushed to the roots of her blue-white hair as she
shovelled the ices into the brown paper bag. 'It's only
sometimes the traveller has them,' she said.

I don't know what they put in the chocolate to make
it so cold and soft on the tongue, but it almost helped.
I went to Matthews to buy a new packet of coloured
pencils even though I didn't need them.

I wanted to walk among the art materials, the tubes
of paint with vivid names. Raw Umber, Grenadine, Sap
Green, Lamp Black. The special pens for calligraphy,
pastel crayons so soft, fairy-tale blue, pink, yellow, the
beautiful rich creamy cartridge paper that I would
never get to use. Because I couldn't draw to save my
life.

I stumbled over to the boring student section with
the compasses, graph paper, set squares, but as I did
something flashed past my eye. A packet of coloured
pencils for children. Noah and his wife with her hand
on her hips, their sons Shem, Ham and Japheth, elephants, giraffes, camels, tigers, lions. They were all

smiling in front of their rainbow which had twelve colours, each colour corresponding to one of the pencils in the packet.

I bought the packet and ran all the way home to draw the lymphatic system. Two new shades of yellow. Perhaps a bit of orange here and there for contrast.

I skimmed along the back streets behind the courthouse, half crying, half laughing. Singing a raucous punky song that I'd just made up about Shem, Ham and Japeth.

I did little skips and the tops of the buildings bumped up and down in time to my original chorus when I ran straight into someone's chest. Someone with long hair and an army jacket. Fred's voice. 'Jesus, you're in great form, Maeve!'

I was so mortified I'd have agreed to anything. I couldn't look at his face. I looked at the sky darkening to violet. There was a colour for that in Matthews. Lake Violet. Oh yes. Eight o'clock, I'd be ready for the seance, I said. Had he heard me?

I slunk home like a dog to plead with Ger. I was going to lay all the blame on Fred. He was gone mad. Frightened me into it with his wild orphan eyes and hungry pleading. Everyone was looking at me on the street. I had to pacify him.

But Ger wasn't at the flat and I couldn't find my key. I finished the chocolate ices on the front doorstep as I sat waiting for Ger. Noah looked pathetic now. If I couldn't draw there was no point in lusting after art materials. *The expense of it!* Noah's white beard looked coarse, his face was beaming no longer. His mouth was outraged like my father's. *The sheriff will be knocking on the door. We'll all be out on the side of the road!*

I picked up my rucksack and walked up to college to look for Ger. She was in the reading rooms reading a book about American Indians. It wasn't on her course but she saw it in the library and ever since Pierce had loaned her *Bury My Heart at Wounded Knee*, she'd wanted to know more.

I thought about drawing Indians and all the browns and rusts and fawns I'd get to use, but I put that thought firmly out of my head. Ger nodded absently to my story about Fred. She said that she would follow me home later. I was afraid she hadn't registered that we were having a seance and would be mad later so I began to tell her about Fred again.

'He wants to follow his parents to the grave. He said that he'd raise them up, he didn't care the price.'

Ger cut me short. 'Wouldn't you think that that brother the fat doctor would do something, give him an injection or get him admitted out of our bloody way.'

'Well he was still fairly sane,' I said quickly.

'Look, I want to finish this, I've got to get *Madame Bovary* done before the end of the week as well.'

Ger didn't give one damn about me or Fred. Mad or not. I felt a bit cross, leaving the reading rooms. Forgot that I'd been meaning to stay and do some study. Trying to scan the room from under my eyelashes, telling myself that I wasn't really looking round for Carl. And how did Ger know that Fred's brother was fat? She'd never met him, had she? If she knew him well she might feel she had to warn him about Fred's insanity.

Back at the flat, I got out *The Plant Kingdom*. I should really have been looking at something I hated. Like a physics problem.

I wasn't thinking of Carl and I was really getting something done, when the doorbell went. I could see the shape of Fred. Long lean army-jacket chest, a few strands of long hair. Could his brother have been on to him so soon? I opened the door.

'Fred, I'm sorry!'

'You're grand, everything under control. I brought a few bottles, but we need to cut out the letters before the others arrive.'

'What others?'

'I just invited a couple from the college bar.'

I wondered who the couple were. I didn't think I knew *any* couple. I supposed that they were some old couple, Fred's age. Demonstrators. I hoped that they hadn't done any demonstrating to me.

I started to help Fred but he said that I was cutting the letters all wrong so I cooked him a poached egg on toast to make up for all the terrible things I'd said about him. I'd guessed that he kept doing seances because his parents were dead and he missed them. But he'd never spoken about them to me.

'How did your parents die?' I asked as he was cutting his egg into little squares.

'Car crash.' He kept chewing and he didn't seem upset, so I left it there. Although I regretted having asked him the question when he was chewing. I wondered how old he was when they died. It was so sad really, I supposed, and tried to imagine my own parents getting killed. A dark flame sprang up inside me. I tried to push it down but it wouldn't go away. Getting all their money and land, Carl at the funeral and getting rid of them for ever as well. *I suppose you'll be dancing on my grave yet. Laughing at me. Don't think you'll get a penny. The farm is mortgaged up to the hilt. Anything that's left will go to your cousin Sean, breaking his back here every summer.*

He was an awful liar so you never knew how much he had, but my cousin had been angling and his farm joined ours and he was a man so my father was probably right about that. It didn't stop me from wishing that he was dead. My heart racing. *You'll have no luck for it!*

· Six ·

I had a lot of reasons to fear a seance, the useless life I was leading, the things I'd said about Fred behind his back. The painless instant death I was planning for my parents. But I was on a reckless wave of hysteria, and when Fred offered me a cigarette I took it. Even though I'd been really trying to keep off them in case I met Carl.

The hard smoke of cigarettes was ruining the chocolatey scent of my fingers. I inhaled harder and waved the smoke away from the front of my face.

'You're nervous, aren't you?' Freddie's green khaki arm suddenly shot around my back. He didn't know that I didn't know how to cope with light-hearted embraces. So it wasn't his fault that I got confused, turned around and burned his fingers with the cigarette.

It was only a brush but he ran shouting into the bathroom as if he'd been disembowelled.

'I'm sorry.' I stood outside the bathroom feeling guilty and mad. Mad because Fred could have made light of the burn if he really wanted to. Spared my feelings a bit.

'I'm sorry,' I said again, over the cold shivery sound of the tap running, wondering if maybe it *was* a bad burn. A third-degree burn. I might have to bring him to hospital.

The water stopped. Fred's boots clumped towards the door and opened it. He stood in the doorway, dabbing at his hand with my small white towel that was specially for my face. He'd soaked the corner in cold water.

'It's alright, it's alright girl, I never knew your nerves were that bad.' But it was too late for him to be magnanimous when I was trying hard to forgive him for using my towel.

It looked like the seance was going to go ahead after all.

'What age were you when your parents were killed?'
'Twelve.'

Did Fred's eyes look wet or was it my imagination? Dab, dab, went the towel, grey marks like wreathes of cigarette smoke moving across my snowy towel. What was I going to use to dry my face tonight? The atmosphere was uneasy, Fred creaking from one foot to the other in his hippy boots. I think even Fred was going off the idea of the seance when the doorbell went.

'It's that couple of demonstrators,' I said and went to the door.

Fred called after me, 'What demonstrators?' and I opened the door to Carl and Tom, Carl's black plastic coat shimmering like the sea at night.

I knew then that Carl and Tom were the couple that Fred had invited. I would have been pleased if that fatal cigarette hadn't been bothering me. I addressed all my questions to Tom even though I didn't want to.

'Best is parking the car, but he's not staying. He's doing a gig in the college bar with Manslaughter.' Carl wore brilliant tight black trousers like something a bullfighter would wear. I stared at them as he walked over to the window to watch Best manoeuvring. His coat shimmered even more, nearly blinding me.

Tom stood beside Fred saying 'Hey man' and other hippy things to annoy him. I crept over to the window and stood beside Carl, but I couldn't bear to talk to him. I stared intently as if Best's straining torso and twisted bumblebee head was all I ever wanted to gaze at.

When Best leaped out of the car I noticed that he had new shiny steel toecaps like Jimmy Barry. I went to the front door but he was kicking at it before I got it opened. Fred tried to give Best a withering look but it was no good when Fred was such a weak-looking sapling, swaying over the table drawing letters on cardboard. I sat down and helped him, annoyed with the way Carl and Tom were standing around just looking.

There was a horrible air in the room since Best had arrived and I could see that Fred was doing his best to get control of things.

'Right, look if you want this to work, you just have to obey a few simple rules, firstly . . .'

'Jesus Fuck! Rules!' Best threw a kick at the table and ruined the beautiful symmetrical X I was inscribing so carefully. I was surprised that Carl and Tom didn't tell him to cop himself on, but they seemed thrilled with him. The sound of screeching brakes and Best shouting 'Manslaughter' turned my Z into another scrawl.

Although Manslaughter were hardly known as a band, they were the most famous people in Cork. We rushed to the window to watch them doing a war dance in the garden. They had hatchets and we couldn't hear them but you could see by their mouths that they were going 'Hiya, hiya, hiya' like Indians. They wore chain mail and they had neat bright red and green stripes on their shaved heads. Best couldn't possibly have banged out the front door harder and we could hear Manslaughter wailing as Fred's hair lifted in the draught.

Silence fell except for the sound of Fred cutting out the letters. He was using the new scissors that Ger had bought for trimming her hair. *And hair only,* Ger had said. *Cutting paper ruins scissors.* Ger knew this because her mother was a dressmaker. I was praying Fred would have the letters done before Ger arrived. I didn't tell him to hurry because he'd only want to know why and that would delay things further. I jumped at every sound thinking it was Ger's footsteps.

He'd barely put the scissors down on the table when I picked them up and took them back to the cutlery drawer. As I fired the scissors into the drawer, there was a rustling sound in the corner of the kitchen. It looked like the refuse bag was slumping and readjusting itself even though it was hours since I'd touched it. I ran back into the other room.

The others gave me a funny stare.

'Did you move that rubbish bag in the kitchen?' I asked Fred and the three of them looked at me as if I was mental.

'Everyone sit with their hands close but not touching.' I was glad there was to be no contact, I couldn't stand it if Carl touched me. Not after I'd smoked that stupid fag.

'What about Ger?' I asked. 'Shouldn't we wait for her?'

Fred gave me a furious look. 'Secondly, concentrate on nothing.'

'That's a bit of a tall order!' Carl said.

'Toner, keep quiet.' Fred had latched on to Carl's

45

surname in an attempt to keep him under control. 'Look at a dot on the ceiling, focus on something, anything. Try to empty your mind. Thirdly no one must speak. There's nothing worse than stupid talk for driving spirits away. Actually don't look at a dot.' Carl was leaning back with his chair on two legs to stare at a damp patch on the ceiling. 'Close your eyes and *think* of the spot.'

'But how will we see the glass moving?' Tom asked.

'Shit!' shouted Fred. 'You're driving me fucking mad! Sorry, look everyone place their right index finger, or left if you're left-handed, over the glass. Don't close your eyes, forget about spots and just fucking *concentrate!*'

We were as good as gold, Fred beseeched the spirits and still nothing happened.

'I'm sick of this.' Tom pushed his chair back.

'You're such a fool, did you think it would be this easy?' Fred asked.

Tom pulled his chair in again and Fred kept calling. Half an hour went by. I concentrated so hard I thought that I was going to get a black-out. The room moved around me.

Tom took his finger down and began to rub his elbow impatiently. I was sure then that I heard a moan coming from the kitchen door, but nobody else moved an eye so I let on nothing. Then it came louder. I could see Carl's gold eyelashes sweeping like search-lights as a scraping sound came from the kitchen door. I held my breath so hard I had to let it go suddenly and scattered the letters. 'Calm down, Maeve,' Fred said.

'It's alright, I think it's a dog,' Carl said.

The dog's nails clipped along the lino. He was a black smooth-haired terrier and he looked unfriendly.

He stared at us with his black nose pointing like a double-barrelled shotgun.

Then the front door banged and made me jump again as the sound of running footsteps came to the door of the flat. A key scratched in the lock and Ger burst in, her hair untidy, half covering her face. 'Has anyone seen a dog?'

'It's useless, I give up. We can't go on with all these interruptions.' Fred began to tidy up the letters.

'Oh don't,' Ger said. 'I just brought him home because he was starving. Wait until I give him some Weetabix, I'm dying to see something.'

'So are we,' muttered Carl.

Ger ran into the kitchen, sending a cold draught through the room and came out with an old bowl, breaking the Weetabix up as she went to the sofa where the dog had settled himself, brazen as anything.

'Isn't it weird the way he went round the back as if he knew?' Ger asked us and we all stared at her, half dizzy from silence and concentration.

The dog put his head on her lap and closed his eyes comfortably. I could hear the sound of Ger's palms rubbing against the dog's rough coat.

'It's not working,' Fred said after about five minutes. 'Something isn't right, I can feel it.'

'Why doesn't Ger come in to the circle?' Carl asked.

At first Ger didn't want to, she said that the dog was comfortable and she didn't want to disturb him. And when she finally agreed she seemed just sorry for us. The dog was savage. Tried to stop her getting out from under him. Stared after her from the couch with outraged human eyes.

I was so sick of it. My right arm was aching and I had to prop it up with my left one. At first I wasn't sure the glass was moving, sliding oh so slowly until I heard Carl's quick intake of breath and saw Fred reach for his pencil and pad. I didn't take my eyes off the glass but I could feel the way everyone was looking. The wonder. I could see the tremor in Tom's hand from the corner of my eye. At first the letters made no sense. I thought that maybe they were anagrams we had to work out, but then in what seemed only a short time the glass began to move faster, steadier. Made words.

Maybe if we'd contacted Fred's parents or something I might have been convinced we were connected to a world beyond. But Short Bull for god's sake! Ger had read the good bits of *Bury My Heart at Wounded Knee* aloud to me when she'd got it that time from Pierce. Now I couldn't believe the way that she didn't think I'd notice. And then it was a string of Indian names: Short Bull, Running Water, Kicking Bear, finishing up with The Great I Am.

I couldn't believe in them and they told us nothing. Announced their names and that was it. No advice or help for the exams. Tom and Carl hardly spoke, they just watched real hard. I was trying to figure out how the glass was flying around so quick and were Fred and Ger in league. The dog kept scratching passionately and staring at each of us in turn, pointing his double-barrelled nose rudely.

Everyone else was taking it seriously and Carl tried to stop me from looking under the table. Of course Carl and Tom were taken in because they didn't know about *Bury My Heart at Wounded Knee*. I tried to catch Ger's eye but she was concentrating hard. There was a tiny line of moisture on the top of her lip that nearly convinced me.

I still couldn't figure out how she was doing it, when

I heard a low chuckle from the sofa. Nobody else noticed, but when I looked at the dog he was yawning nonchalantly, his teeth like stalactites and stalagmites in the pink cave of his mouth. I felt a shiver just under my ribcage and then the noise in the kitchen began.

At first I thought it was the refuse bag sliding again.

'Did you come back this evening to put rubbish in that bag?' I asked Ger and she gave me the same puzzled look that the others gave me before.

'There is something in the kitchen,' I said. 'I know there is. It could be a rat, oh god, why isn't our kitchen a bit cleaner!'

The others still stared.

'Can't you hear that tapping noise?' Everyone kept still and the noise stopped.

I threw open the kitchen door, expecting them all to follow me. I ran to the corner where the refuse sack stood but it was perfectly motionless. Then the tapping came again and I turned around to see the kettle hopping up and down on the cooker. When I touched it, it was boiling hot. I jumped back, dropping the handle and it spat a few drops in my hand.

The others only came out when I screamed. When it was too late for them to bear witness. They said that I was overwrought, that the success of the seance was too much for me.

'Don't make me laugh,' I said, but when I saw Fred's face it was obvious that he too was taken in. I couldn't make up my mind about Ger. Could she have managed to trick us all single-handed? I didn't mention *Bury My Heart at Wounded Knee* because I didn't want to embarrass her. I was sure I'd have a burn on my hand but there was nothing.

'Feel, Maeve,' Ger said. 'The kettle is stone cold.'

The cold metal made me shiver – it felt like it was a long time since it had been boiled.

I kept wishing that our kitchen was cleaner. In front of Carl. His beautiful bullfighting trousers disappearing out the door and Ger saying no we were fine we didn't want a drink and course Maeve would be fine, wasn't she going to look after me herself?

· *Seven* ·

'Talk about giving up your golden chance,' Ger said when the door closed behind Fred, Tom and Carl. 'Why didn't you say you'd go to Curtains!'

I didn't answer. She had made it impossible for me to go, speaking for the two of us. Saying we were fine and we needed an early night.

'I thought you'd grab the opportunity when I said I wanted to stay in and study,' said Ger.

What kind of an actress was she? Sounding so concerned. And why was she so complacent about staying on at the flat? Why wasn't Ger scared if she thought that the seance had worked?

'Oh at least we won't have to be putting up with Mad Myra,' Ger said.

The dog didn't want to go when Ger pushed him through the doorway. He moaned so sadly I begged her to let him stay.

'What if his owners are looking for him?'

'They should have fed him properly.'

'Just tonight. You know we can't risk it with that bloody landlord sneaking in all the time.'

At bedtime, I ran back to the kitchen to give the dog an old blanket. He was trying to forage in the refuse sack. It was moving like mad now and I supposed it would have to be since he was wrestling with it. Ger helped me to put it outside the front door and it gave one last little rustle as we were shutting the door. I jumped again and Ger told me I was tired.

Then there was a rumbling sound from the kitchen and we both heard it. Running up the stairs took forever. My legs were heavy, like trying to escape in a dream. Ger didn't stop to investigate either. When we got into our bedroom, I said to Ger maybe it was just the boiler or the washing machine next door.

'It's bound to be the dog,' said Ger, but we left the lights on and the gas fire burning downstairs. My father's voice in my head, *go on, go on, do your level best to break me, drive me into an early grave before I end up in Queer Street.*

I couldn't stay on my own, I wanted to sleep with Ger, but Ger said no way could she go to sleep with the lights on so we turned them off and opened the curtains to let in the street-lamps; two orange moons, one big and one little because it was on the other side of the street.

When I asked her, Ger said that she couldn't smell any cigarette smoke from me, all she could smell was chocolate, and then we discovered that I'd a flattened melted chocolate ice in the back pocket of my jeans. If only I'd known I could have sat closer to Carl. Maybe even put my leg right up against his tight bullfighter trousers.

The noises seemed to stop for a while. I fell into a light sleep but then I started awake at a thud and Ger woke up at the same time.

'That bloody dog!' Ger said. 'He'll wreck the place!'

'Should we chuck him out?' I asked.

'I'm too tired,' Ger said and I said that I was too.

I wondered if we should get a priest in to bless the place, and then I figured we couldn't because our flat was too dirty. Ger only snorted at the thought of a priest. She said that she'd had enough of priests when she was growing up because her mother was so religious and very near to being a widow. I wondered what that meant. I had thought that she *was* a widow.

The noises stopped when Ger talked about her family. I got in beside Ger and as she talked we smoked, golden fingers flying to our mouths, inhaling and exhaling at the same time.

I looked at the way Ger's fingers tapered around her cigarette and waited for her to go on.

'My mother has this superstition about putting anything important in a letter. In case it gets into the wrong person's hands. She's got all these dramatic stories about people going through the ground in other people's houses when they saw their personal letters thrown open on sideboards and bedside lockers for every Tom, Dick and Harry to be reading. Disasters always follow. Engagements broken off, people written out of wills and all that kind of stuff.'

I thought guiltily of my father's will and listened for the bumps. It was quiet now, no sound apart from deep sighs as we dragged on our cigarettes.

'She wouldn't write to my father,' Ger went on. 'All this martyrdom and "don't put anything in a letter that you wouldn't like anyone else to read". Instead of telling him to get his arse back to Ireland to look after his six young children and to have less of the fantasies about Kit Burke down the road intercepting the letter and broadcasting it across the parish. As if the whole country didn't know that he was never with us.'

'Where was he?'

'He went to England to look for work and never stayed with her for more than a month after that. They still managed to have six girls and I'm the eldest. I'm supposed to be responsible. My mother never said a word against him. Just prayed harder and worked harder at her looks. She was gorgeous in the sixties, hair and suits and little gloves like Jackie Kennedy. He did send her money, and besides she could make her own clothes, really beautiful stuff for half nothing.'

'She sounds really fantastic.'

'She's a fucking eedjit. Full of shame and worrying about Kit Burke, stoned out of her mind about my father. I reckon it was because she hardly ever saw him. It made him seem mysterious. I thought he was mysterious and fantastic too when I was a child. The scales fell from my eyes when I was about fifteen and I realised he was an even bigger eedjit only selfish as well.'

'He could have had mysterious problems,' I said charitably.

Another snort from Ger followed by a sarcastic curl of smoke. 'He made us call him Joe. He didn't like Daddy he said. I remember meeting him at the railway station and he used to have narrow-legged suits, his hair combed back and those cute little sixties overcoats that came just over his knees. Later on he became a bit smarmy looking, long peaks on his shirt collars almost sweeping his growing stomach. Tight sheepskin coats with gloves to match. That's when he became an auctioneer.'

'An auctioneer!' I exclaimed.

Ger didn't snort when I cut in this time, she just looked at me sadly. 'The last time he came home was 1974. We were very excited. He hired a car just to

54

drive us to look at a farm five miles away. Parked the car two miles from the farm because he said we needed exercise. Even though he was the one with the fat stomach. We were all pure needles then, especially my mother. She didn't even eat meat. She said we needed it more because our brains were still growing. She just ate boiled eggs and Ryvita with Blue Band margerine. We all had ringlets except for my mother who was wearing a second-hand green silk headscarf that one of her customers had passed on. You'd never know it wasn't new. She looked just like Edna O'Brien. Joe had a face like a knife when I told him where she'd got the scarf. One look at my mother's face and I knew I'd said the wrong thing.'

'What happened?'

'He snatched the scarf off my mother's head. She looked completely flattened in every way as she walked up the road ahead of us. He looked like Heathcliff, muttering under his shaggy hair.

'We were going to look at a farm that was up for sale. Joe wanted to come home with all his money and settle down in a real Irish home. He was big into being Irish and making sure that we were being brought up innocent in the Irish countryside. Irish. Irish. Irish. It's an excuse for everything.'

I couldn't be sure in the lamplight but Ger's face seemed to have gone greeny pale. I wondered if she knew that she was frightening me. She put the cigarette out quickly on the floor beside our bed. Her stomach heaved as if she wanted to get sick. I wanted to ask her if she was alright but I couldn't because her face was so angry. There wasn't a sound from downstairs. I wondered what position the dog was sleeping in.

Ger came round after about half a minute. 'It was

June. Hot. Bees and flies humming. I can still smell the grass and the sharper smell of the nettles. I had to watch my little sisters because they didn't have the sense to avoid the nettles. They were so young then. I hated to see their white skin all puckered and bright pink with stings. And no matter how much dock-leaf juice I squeezed over the stings, it never seemed to give them any relief.

'We were picking foxgloves and putting them on our fingers. Stopping to make daisy chains and then running like mad to catch up. My scalp was itchy and tingly from the tight ringlets. I held my hands out in front of me to make sure my foxgloves didn't fall off as I ran. My youngest sister Ina sat down on the road and started crying. My mother came back and picked her up.

'There was no one at the old farmhouse and we went around peering in the windows. The rooms were big, we could see a big open fire in the kitchen.

'Joe was thrilling the whole lot of us going on about how we'd be sitting round a blazing fire in the winter, playing forty-five. Going whooo whooo to Ina, making her scream with happiness, showing her how the wind would howl around the house when we'd be safe inside like the three little pigs. I can still see him, his sheep-skin coat over his arm, little drops of sweat across his forehead. I even thought his sweat was glamorous. Of course we weren't used to men. We ran all around the house. There was a stream at the back and an orchard with pear trees, apple trees and rusty farm machinery. Joe boasting to beat the band. *I'll get that orchard really going. Who'll give me a hand to clear the rubbish?* Winking at me. The lazy old bastard.

'There was a paddock with grass up to Ina's waist. Joe said that he was going to put six Shetland ponies into the paddock. My mother's face looked like she was doing the Stations of the Cross. I could see that she was deadly ashamed of the way she was hoping. Nearly as bad as putting something important in a letter.

'We peered in the windows, shielding our faces to keep the shadows out of our view. In one room we could see a marble fireplace with black and white tiles. There were little naked angels on the tiles. Joe said they were like us. He was going to name the angels after us. Geraldine, Teresa, Carmel, Rose, Susie and Ina. Rose and Susie were delighted. They're the twins.'

I shivered a bit when Ger mentioned the angels, I thought for a minute she was talking about real ones.

'There were french windows leading from the parlour out into a small garden with a tiny low hedge. Even the twins could jump over it. Ina tried to jump over it too, but she fell and got stuck. We were all so excited she forgot to cry.

'*Imagine walking out of the parlour on a summer's evening*, I remember Joe saying and my mother's face lighting up slowly. Falling in love with it in the middle of all her shame and humility. *Just a few old-fashioned rose-bushes*. But that wasn't enough for Joe. Oh no! He was going to have fuschia all around. Rhododendrons coming up the drive, apple trees, rambling roses, Virginia creeper, pear trees, big daisies, plum trees. Raspberries, gooseberries, the works. My mother of course making tarts and jams and pickles and flowery curtains for every window. The smell of brown bread baking in the oven every morning. He was going to get someone in to paint the whole place white inside and out. Our own potatoes, carrots, lettuce, eggs, my mother rearing the hens and us collecting the eggs. We'd never have to go near a shop. When he started on to asparagus, my mother's face was a panic. God would strike us all dead! Who did we think we were! And I was half worried too, the way he was throwing Ina around the air. She was screaming so much I thought her asthma would come back.

'We ran all the way to the car, it was getting cool and you couldn't smell the nettles any more. The midges were out now and we were all scratching our ringlets. Joe had Ina on his back and he was singing *we'll go no more a roving*.

'He sang loads of songs on the way back, "Kevin Barry", "Botany Bay", "Boolavogue", "Tonight We're Going to Free Old Wexford Town". When we got back, my mother sang "The Kerry Races" and Joe was rubbing her neck the whole time she was singing. I sang "An Maidrin Rua", I'd only just learnt it at school that week.

'Joe helped Teresa to put her daisies into a whiskey glass full of water. Their pink heads were closing and the thin stems crossing each other, moving slightly as if they were treading the water.'

Ger stopped for a moment to cough. 'He never came back after that visit. My mother even stopped going to Mass for a while. But nothing worked.

'Ina and my mother still expect him to come back, even though someone else owns the farm now. It's a stud farm. Big business and no romance. Women in jodhpurs and cruel expensive-looking polished boots. I try not to notice them. What kills me most is I know if he turned up even now Ina and my mother would have a big welcome for him.'

'Oh that's desperate,' I said, thinking that I'd love to meet Ger's father. He was away more interesting than Sitting Bull and Running Water.

Later I thought that I heard the sound of glass breaking and I woke Ger up even though I'd tried my hardest to be brave on my own.

Ger was really mad. 'That dog is getting door first thing tomorrow morning.'

'What if it isn't the dog?' I asked.

Ger said that she found it very hurtful the way I was deliberately trying to frighten and upset her. She threw back the satin eiderdown and rushed out of the room wearing nothing but a T-shirt. I could hear her bare feet angry, thumping each stair as she went down. I could hear the dog whimpering and objecting as she pushed him out. The front door slamming. Ger came back wiping what seemed to be tears from her face.

· *Eight* ·

We slept late, woke up sheepish with each other. It was hard now to believe the way we had felt the night before. We did a few rushed apologies out of embarrassment. Said everything that happened was our imagination.

Ger's imagination I was sure. We spent the whole day in college. I did a pile of botany drawings, even got hopeful about my scientific chances. Ger read half of *Madame Bovary* as well as going to all her lectures and two tutorials. Walking home at nine o'clock that night, we were triumphant. Magnanimous to the beggars who suddenly appeared on the bridge outside Jury's Hotel.

Then we met that dog from the seance. He cooled our blood. Pointing the barrel of his nose at us. Ger went half hysterical, shouting 'Go home, go home!'

He looked at her before turning away slowly.

'I thought you liked him,' I said.

'Go home,' Ger shouted again and he loped off uncertainly. I doubted that he had any home to go to.

'Not that much.' Ger recovered quickly, said that she'd never be superstitious like her mother. As we walked on down the street, she told me one of her mother's stories. It was half killing her to tell it, so she kept putting in sarcastic bits to show that she wasn't taken in.

'Every morning this girl went to early Mass. She was beautiful as well as holy. Only beautiful people get into my mother's stories. This girl anyway, fierce religious, wore Chanel suits, had a handbag with a golden chain.' Ger's words were cynical, but the whites of her eyes rolled wildly and her face in the twilight was dark green like ivy. 'A black dog barred her path!' Ger stopped dead.

'Go on!'

'Well, I can't remember, oh yes, the priest happened to come along at the same time. She was early or he was late for some reason.' Ger seemed ashamed of herself for even repeating the story.

'And?'

'The dog was never seen again. Being the devil, he couldn't bear the sight of a priest.' Ger hung her head, looking mortified.

'She could have swung that gold chain and hit him with the handbag,' I joked to relieve Ger.

We were laughing away at the Chanel suit and the golden chain, when, up the road, the dog passed us again, and went to sniff at Ger's hand.

'Aaaaah,' Ger screamed, and even though I wasn't that frightened I ran fast after Ger towards Curtains.

'He was probably only looking for more Weetabix,' I said.

'Fuck that,' said Ger and crashed the door of Curtains right against the wall, which wasn't a bit like her.

Pierce Curtain was behind the bar. He straightened up when he saw Ger, pulled his shoulders back, gave a quick flick to his hair. Ger didn't notice this because she was trying to get her long black hair out of her eyes.

61

I thought that Pierce was kind of handsome for his age, in an old hippy sort of way, but Ger said that he was pure cat. I elbowed in between a load of raucous engineers, who seemed to be flaming, but they were all drinking rock shandies because the exams were coming up. I tried to get Pierce's attention. He usually served us straight away, but he was watching Ger with a strange hidden expression on his face.

Someone tapped my shoulder. I turned around, sure it was Carl.

But it was only Fred. 'Come on, let me get these. It's the least I can do.'

'Go away, Fred,' I said. 'On top of everything now, we're being followed by that black dog.'

Pierce reached under the counter for two bottles of cider. 'That's for yourself and Ger, and they're from me.'

Fred seemed to be hoping for a free drink too, but Pierce said nothing about that. 'Okay, Pierce, I'll just have a Carlsberg.'

'That'll be seventy pence to you.' He took the fiver from Fred. 'You all look like you've seen a ghost and Ger is shivering. Has she got a cold or what?'

I looked over at the table where Ger was talking to Tom and Carl. Her shoulders were shaking inside the brown coat and she was dragging like mad on her cigarette.

'Well, actually,' I got on my toes and whispered to Pierce, 'we had a seance!'

'A seance!' Pierce's eyebrows dived up. 'Whose idea was that? In that awful creepy flat with those draughty glass doors! You'll frighten yourselves to death.'

Fred's mouth went into a silent whistle and I was wondering too how Pierce was so familiar with our draughty glass doors.

'It worked, you know.'

'Of course it worked! I only have to look at you to know it worked!'

Fred looked furtive, standing there with a moustache of Carlsberg still sitting on his upper lip from the first sip.

'It'll be alright,' he said in a stupid placatory voice.

'Alright? Alright?' Pierce raised his voice and a load of people looked at us. 'How're those two girls going to go back to that flat tonight? Look at the condition of them!'

I was annoyed with that. I thought I was looking kind of well.

Freddie didn't say anything, just kept gulping Carlsberg until he was halfway down the glass, his Adam's apple going up and down.

'Look, Maeve, if you want to stay here, you know you're welcome. You can't go back to that place if you're terrified. Myra will be only delighted, you know that.'

I took the drinks from the counter and turned towards Ger's table. 'Thanks, Pierce, but I'm sure that we'll be fine.'

'There's no need for bravado in front of me,' Pierce called after me. A crowd of girls drinking orange juice stared at me as I went through the crowd. I recognized some of them from chemistry practicals and hung my head.

Things looked good at first. Tom and Carl had joined our table. Then I looked at Ger, her brows were knitted and she gave me a weird look. 'What's he saying, for god's sake, everyone's looking at you!'

'He's saying nothing.'

'He's saying something, you'd better tell me what it

is.' Ger was like a demon, staring out from under her brows.

'I just told him about the seance . . .'

'You what?'

'Well, we always tell Pierce things. Don't we?'

'No, *I* don't. You do!'

'What's wrong with that? He says we can stay with him and Myra for the night.'

'*He what?*' Tom and Carl started as Ger pounded a tin of tobacco on the table and stalked across the lounge towards the toilets. The girls drinking orange juice stared as she went past, her shabby brown coat swinging.

Pierce saw Ger and raised a hand in greeting, but she must have cut him because he turned back to a customer, his face full of dismay.

'What's wrong with her? She's like a fucking Antichrist!' Tom lit a cigarette and inhaled.

'Look what she's been through, last night. Being used as a medium by that . . . that whatever it was.' I pressed my knees together. They were shaking so hard I was afraid that they'd bang the table.

'I thought you were the medium,' Carl said, and gave me a nudge. I didn't know whether I should get annoyed or not because I'd really enjoyed the nudge.

'Hey, come on a minute,' Tom said.

'No, it wasn't deliberate, it was just Maeve's unconscious.'

'It was Ger. *Her* unconscious.' I was driven to defend myself. 'I know for a fact that she was reading this book all about Indians. The very day of the seance. That's where Sitting Bull and all that crowd came from.'

'I was reading about the Taj Mahal, you eedjit.' The long seat I was sitting on bumped as Ger sat down

64

heavily beside me. She refused to talk to me for the rest of the evening. I knew she was lying, but she was very upset as well and I had been a bit of a traitor.

'The unconscious is deadly,' Carl said. 'That's why I came to the seance really. I'm interested in dream language.'

'I'd love to read a book about it,' I said bravely when I thought Tom wasn't listening.

Before Carl had a chance to answer, a voice said 'Push over, girl!' It was Claire, the medical student. 'I was over there.' She pointed to the crowd of practical scientists drinking orange juice. 'And you walked past me with your head down. I shouted Maeve but you kept going.' Claire put her hand over her mouth and gave a small giggle. Her blonde hair was in a jaunty ponytail and there wasn't a single crease on her snowy grandfather shirt.

'I didn't see you,' I said.

'I know you didn't.' She began to laugh harder.

I introduced Tom and Carl and she was almost holding her sides. They looked very put out and it must have been hard for them with someone as glamorous as Claire laughing her head off.

Carl wasn't really talking to me now and I remembered how scared I was of going back to the flat. Our bedroom was so cold and there were two huge mirrors hanging over our beds. We had to kneel on our pillows to put on our eyeliner. Brown spots covered my reflection. When I wanted to see a reflection of my face in one piece, I had to go to the toilets in the science block. Ger's mirror was worse. There was a discoloured mushroom-shaped mark around the level of my mouth. When Ger looked in the mirror, the mark was over her throat. As if she'd been mauled.

Best came in. I couldn't believe it but he was with

Jimmy Barry. They were talking, laughing, joshing each other. And there was a really weird-looking fellow called Murphy with them wearing bondage trousers and a tight-fitting stripy T-shirt. Muscles poured out of his T-shirt. He had orangey-yellow spiky hair and a mouth like a trap. I was waiting for them all to get up and start beating the hell out of each other.

'Jimmy Barry's the new bass player,' Carl told me in a dazed voice.

Best and Jimmy Barry kept boasting about how worn out they were and I asked Murphy what had they been doing.

Murphy grinned like a shark. 'They're worn out from expressing their personalities.'

'Doing what?' Claire managed between another huge fit of laughing.

'Doing wrecky.'

'What's doing wrecky?' I asked.

'That one hasn't a fucking breeze,' Jimmy Barry said and nudged my boots with his steely toecaps. 'The punk who can't gob!'

'Tell 'em all to fuck off!' Murphy said and put a hard muscly arm around my shoulder. 'Hey,' he said to Carl, 'I thought that she was your missus, you should be minding her!'

'I don't need minding,' I said quickly, terrified that Carl would deny I was his missus.

Jimmy Barry pointed his lemon face at Carl. 'Are you on then?'

'Of course I'm on.' Carl kept folding his monkey hat. Best was grinning.

'Were you at the Arc the other night?' Murphy asked me.

'I was.' I drooped at the memory.

'I know! What a fucking disappointment. They've

sold out alright boy. I mean Top of the fucking Pops.'
Murphy spat from the side of his mouth in disgust. I
moved my boots quickly. 'D'ya ever hear of Beel-
zebubba!'

I jumped, my heart zigzagging round my chest.
'Where? Where?'

'Calm down, girl, I've only got the record.'

'Oh, a band!'

'There's some great tracks. "My Many Smells".
"Punk Rock Girl". Fucking dynamite!'

'Oh I don't know much, I'm not really a punk.'

Murphy didn't contradict me even though I was
hoping like mad. 'I'll lend ya the album all the same.
I'd say you'd go for it, alright.'

I was getting annoyed with Claire for laughing
because it was very distracting for Carl. Best was staring
at her and saying tough things to Jimmy Barry, but
Claire only laughed more. She kept wiping her eyes
with her perfectly ironed blue and white striped man's
handkerchief.

'I like your snot rag,' Best was saying, driving her
even worse.

Ger was sulking and blowing smoke into Tom's face.
Tom was trying to pretend the smoke wasn't in his
eyes. 'Will you have another bottle?' he asked me,
his eyes streaming.

'There isn't time,' I said.

I could see Pierce lifting up the counter. I knew he
was coming out to clear us.

'What's this about wrecky?' I asked Carl.

'I must get a pair of bondage trousers when I go to
London.' Carl's grey eyes were distant. I couldn't
figure out whether he was pretending to be fascinated
with the leather straps that bridged the gap between

the two legs of Murphy's trousers, or whether he just didn't want to explain wrecky.

'Are ye jagging or not?'

I went red when Murphy asked the question and Carl started whistling.

Murphy got up to go with Jimmy Barry. 'Ye need to break loose from yer chains. I know about these things, I'm an existentialist.'

'Keep away from that looney,' said Jimmy Barry, referring to me as he buttoned up his duffle coat. His face looked wooden, sinister when he pulled his hood up.

'Tell me when ye want to break loose,' Murphy said, as he picked up his toolbox.

My mouth was swinging like a hammock. I think Carl knew what an existentialist was but I hadn't a clue.

· *Nine* ·

Best went with Jimmy Barry and Murphy. We stayed late while Pierce collected glasses. He still looked worried. 'Where's Ger?'

'She's in the toilet.'

'Again? Is she alright?'

'She'll be fine, she just had a bit of a fright,' Tom told Pierce.

'What kind of a fright?' Pierce's brown face went long and dark.

'She was used as a kind of a medium.'

Fred had followed Pierce from the counter and was standing beside him drinking his Carlsberg steadily. Staring at Pierce, as if he was trying to figure him out.

'You can't go back there tonight,' Pierce said. 'Stay here with us, we've plenty of spare rooms.'

'You could stay with me,' Fred offered suddenly. His eyes looked glassy and the skin of his face was stretched and brittle. I felt sorry for him.

'No thanks,' I said and stood up, 'I've got to check Ger.' I moved away quickly because I felt like crying and I didn't want anyone to see my disappointment. Why wasn't Carl offering?

Ger came out, gave Claire a narrow-eyed look, lit another cigarette and finished her pint of cider.

'You better stay the night, here,' Pierce told her and put his hand lightly on her shoulder.

A funny sheen came on Ger's face when Pierce touched her. She agreed without even looking at him. I wondered if the others noticed.

Pierce and Myra lived above the bar. The stairs that led from the pub were cat. Narrow and dingy. But when you got to the first-floor landing, everything changed. The rooms were full of light from the street-lamps, exotic. I imagined that it was like Germany before the war when they had all those exciting parties. Before the Nazis drove all the kind artistic people out. Not that I knew what those parties were like.

The carpets were pale, the curtains were heavy and rich. Myra had plants everywhere. A couple of umbrella plants had got a bit out of hand, wrestling together towards the window. Sinister. Danger coming.

The front room was lined with books, the only thing that Pierce really cared about according to Myra. He had studied English at college, just like Ger. He was always talking about books to Ger. Sometimes he brought her upstairs. Sometimes I went along. Ger said that Myra was delighted that someone else cared about books beside Pierce.

Climbing the stairs after closing time, I listened for the sound of Myra's troubled voice. She never went out. Someone said once that Pierce had to buy everything for her. Even underwear and embarrassing things.

But there was no sound of Myra, just cracking noises from the radiators and floorboards, the far-away hum of the fridge in the kitchen. Pierce crossed the room to draw the curtains, muffling the sound of the street outside. A few of the customers were still gathered

70

below. Their voices rose now and then. Some of them had brought their drinks outside. You could hear the glasses chinking. I thought with a pang that I could still hear Carl's voice.

Slumping sadly into a beanbag, I listened to Pierce talking to Ger.

'Look at this, got it down in the Coal Quay.' He waved a raggedy book at Ger.

Ger still had that sleek look. 'Coleridge,' she sighed and flicked the marbled pages with her pink, cold hands.

It had been such a long night trying to encourage Carl without anyone else noticing. My eyes kept closing. Pierce had to get the sleeping bags in the end. I noticed that he was half apologetic with me. He didn't look at Ger when he said good-night. Ger was lying on the floor already in her sleeping bag, her eyes huge holes in her face under the dim light of the standard lamp.

Ger stared into space for a few seconds after Pierce left. She rubbed her pink hands together in a sad kind of rhythm that made my heart ache.

'I really like Carl,' I whispered.

'I know you do,' Ger laughed quietly, holding her left wrist tightly in her right hand as if she was trying to grab hold of herself.

'Does everyone know?' I asked, anxiously.

'Oh fuck everyone, do your own thing!' Ger let go her wrist and leaned on her elbow. She lit a cigarette and went quiet. I waited for deep wisdom. Some indication of what I should do about Carl. But Ger went into a kind of a trance and stayed silent for a long time. I could hear her breath catching every time she inhaled.

'God, I'm exhausted!' I said, moving back to the

other side of the room, not wanting to be selfish. Even though I felt very selfish. And scared. Ger didn't seem to be affected by the noises in our house at all! And if she wasn't scared it was because *she* was the diabolical agent. Maybe she made up that story about her father. She'd always said that he was dead.

My feet were like cold stones at the bottom of the sleeping bag. When one of them touched my knee it didn't feel like any living thing. Shivering and resentful, I watched the tip of Ger's cigarette moving in the dark until she put it out.

Later, when I was half asleep, I heard Pierce come in. I opened my eyes slightly and saw his big shoulders hunched over Ger who was sitting up facing him, the tip of her dark head just visible at the side of his brown neck. I screwed my eyes tight and tried not to hear their torn breaths getting louder.

After a few minutes, Pierce stood up and went out and Ger turned into the wall in her sleeping bag. I'd a pain in my chest from holding my breath too much.

I lay awake for ages wondering about Myra. Did she know? Maybe that was why she kept taking her hair down and saying that she was a young woman. They said she'd had several nervous breakdowns. Was Ger cruel?

Somehow I must have slept because I jerked awake, sat up shivering with the cold. I remembered the seance and the glass shattering. My heart got a bit wild. Panicking, I called Ger, but there was no answer.

I hobbled across the room in my sleeping bag and lifted Ger's blanket and sleeping bag. My right knee began to twitch like a wild animal in a trap. Ger was gone. I shrugged the sleeping bag off my feet and started for the door.

Down at the end of the wide corridor, light streamed from the street through the open kitchen door. Germany before the war.

I tiptoed down, calling Ger's name in a low whisper, then stopped. Pierce was sitting on a kitchen chair and Ger was sitting on his lap facing him. They were kissing and they didn't see me. They were looking at each other. I could see that Pierce's trousers were open. Ger's pink leg hung down the outside of the chair. They didn't see me stand there, transfixed for a moment before hurrying back to the front room.

In the front room I was completely mental, talking to myself, struggling to get into the sleeping bag quickly. As if Pierce and Ger were going to come chasing after me, demanding that I explain my actions.

I waited and waited for Ger to come back, frightened and angry. Cold too. Pierce had plenty of spare bedrooms, so how come we had to sleep on the floor? Pierce seemed to have turned into some kind of devil. In my head the seance glass kept shattering and Pierce's oily black curls mingled with Ger's black strands.

Eventually Ger came back, shivering a bit. And smoking. She stopped beside my beanbag for a second, then went quietly to her own side of the room. I shut my eyes tightly and made regular breathing sounds.

Ger slipped off to sleep quickly, but I tossed and turned. At one point I got up and stood over Ger, willing her to wake up. Ger's oval face was peaceful, she breathed on, deeply. *She* wasn't afraid.

My feet began to freeze. Afraid that I'd get rooted to the floor, I went back to huddle in my sleeping bag. If Ger wasn't scared, maybe she'd secretly organized the whole thing herself. The seance. The dog.

The thing that really killed me was that Ger could

sleep away and there was I, awake worrying. At six o'clock, Ger seemed to wake by instinct and jumped up, buttoning her blouse and her purple waistcoat.

'Maeve, we'd better go!' she called as she pulled on her thick black stockings. 'We better not hang around.'

I was dropping off and had to wake myself up. The injustice of it! 'Because you don't want Myra to know we were here?'

Ger's face only fell slightly. 'You know?'

'Yes.'

'How?'

'I just guessed,' I said, quickly. An image of Ger's pink leg hanging over the side of the chair came into my mind, but I brushed it quickly away. 'I'm not a complete fool.'

'You're mad, aren't you?' Ger's face was pale and tired looking in the grey light.

I didn't answer. I was afraid to. Narrow-minded petty thoughts kept coming into my mind. I was afraid that I might say them. I rummaged around the room, looking for my donkey jacket.

'Here it is.' Ger held it out and I took it silently. I didn't look at her.

'I'm ready to go now,' I said gruffly, before bending down to check the laces on my boots.

We tiptoed down the stairs, me trying to keep my boots light on the stairs, Ger drooping and sighing. I knew that Ger was feeling sick, but I ignored it. I turned round as Ger was opening the front door. Looking up, I saw Pierce passing the top of the stairs, his arms full of rugs and sleeping bags. For the instant I saw his face. It was grim and bleak. He looked as if he had his teeth clenched. I felt sorry for him, and Ger too, now standing outside, her face slightly green in the early morning. I held Ger's hair back while she got sick in a dustbin. The birds were twittering like mad.

I didn't tell Ger that she drank too much. That Claire had diagnosed her condition as acute alcoholic gastritus. I held her hair back like a discreet maid, not approving of her mistress but supporting her anyway.

Ten

Murphy was singing 'I Want You to Want Me,' and my cold ears were ticking like clocks as I stood in the middle of Clashduv Estate with a brick in my hand. Carl beside me taking aim.

I don't know whether I just wanted to let Jimmy Barry know what I was made of or if it was admiration for Carl. Maybe it was just a last-ditch attempt to be a full-blooded punk.

'I'm no good at sport!' I said, eyeing the window which was miles away. I knew that I couldn't reach it and that was a comfort.

'You're alright, girl,' Murphy said. 'Sure that window is practically beside you. You only have to lob it in.'

'Yes,' I said, glad of the dark hiding my cowardly face.

I stood there for what seemed like ages. All I could think of was my father and the way he drove my mother mental. *If he asks me once more where the Ready Reckoner is I'll go off my game!*

'RAAW!' Murphy gave a strangled roar and shot his arm into the air. That was the signal.

'RAAW!' went Carl and ran forward swinging his

76

arm. The brick sailed over the garden wall and landed about a foot from the window.

'Jesus! Christ! I had it, only my wrist gave at the crucial moment.' Carl looked wild. He threw his leg over the wall and Murphy caught his arm.

'Where ya goin?'

'I want to have another go. That was a false start.'

'One chance and one chance only.' Murphy pushed him back.

I couldn't see Carl's face in the dark. I didn't need to see it to know that he was devastated.

'Come on now, Cronin,' roared Murphy and I took a few steps forward. I wondered if I should go Raaw but I didn't.

'Get your back into it,' Murphy screamed as I was feebly taking aim. Jesus, I didn't want to break anything, but afraid to be seen to be a coward, I swung my arm and tossed the brick wildly upwards.

'Look out,' shouted Carl and pulled me to one side as the brick just missed my head.

I clung on to Carl's arm and I didn't care if Murphy thought we were jagging or not. My nerves moved in bunches up and down my body, the wind cut into my cheeks, I thought my heart would stop and Murphy's voice was breaking with admiration. 'Trying to kill yourself, Jesus you're really mad!'

He thought that I was completely fearless.

'You gave me such a fucking fright,' Carl said and if Murphy hadn't been there I'd have made Carl confess that we were both useless. That we weren't cut out for wrecky.

'Useless cunts,' said Murphy affectionately, and took off at full speed swinging his arm like someone from the Olympics. There was a quiet crack at first and then the sound of the glass shattering.

'Come on!' Murphy gave a few more strangled roars. Shouted things like anarchy and power to the under-classes and up your arse in a hoarse voice as we ran down the road like hunted men. I felt like everything was in slow motion and my Docs were too heavy. I began to slow down, thinking it was all up. Waiting for the heavy hand of a guard or a responsible house-holder. But somehow we got out of the estate. No one followed us.

I wanted to get down on my knees to thank god, say that I was very sorry and that I would never trespass again. Carl was clenching his fist, saying that he had to practise.

Drummonds was a plush pub where med and law students drank. A crowd of them turned round and stared at us, especially at Murphy's sharky face and his bondage trousers. They didn't say anything though. Murphy had that kind of face. His yellow hair and his trap mouth were set like plaster.

They would have said something if we'd been on our own. Carl was always getting attacked because of his skinhead haircut. He had to climb up the railings outside a pub one night to get away from a Bank of Ireland crowd who were going violent at the sight of him.

Tom, Best and Carl had been talking about wrecky all week. Meeting Jimmy Barry and Murphy. Getting advice. They'd been wrecking all the phone boxes along Grand Parade. Using the tools from Murphy's tool-box when their hands were too weak.

Best was in hospital after kicking in a plate-glass window. He'd cut his leg and they'd had to call an ambulance. I'd said that it was a good thing they found a phone box working but they told me that was an old joke. I'd said that I wasn't joking and how else could they have got an ambulance. Best had twelve stitches and was thrilled with himself. He'd looked relieved to be getting a rest from it when we visited him in hospital.

'Ye've got to carry on the work,' he'd told Tom and Carl, lying back against six pillows, his electric circuits spread all over the table in front of him. Tom had laughed but Carl had nodded in an alarming way. He wore his bullfighter trousers all the time now. Murphy was mad about the trousers. He kept offering Carl money for them.

I couldn't understand why Carl was taking the wrecky so seriously. I worried that he might be easily led. *Show me your company and I'll tell you who you are.*

Murphy bought three pints of cider and said, 'Sit down and relax after yer hard work.'

I went red. I could see a law student with a thin cigar raising his eyebrows behind Murphy. People who pretended to be superior were deadly for listening in. I knew this fellow to see. He carried a briefcase, had a thin moustache and was into politics and all that kind of stuff. I saw him when I joined the Fine Gael party my first week in college. It had been a last-ditch attempt to be true to my father. I'd only lasted two sessions even though they didn't laugh at me. I could never understand why. They must have known that I was no asset to any party.

'What about being an exist*enti*list?' I asked carefully. I'd practised pronouncing it with Ger.

'What about existentialism?' Murphy said loudly.

The law student's supercilious face took on a faint smile.

'Right, have you heard of Camus?'

'Albert,' said Carl, knowledgeably.

'Right, Albert.' Murphy took a huge drink of cider right down below the middle of the glass. 'Albert believed in absurdity. That is the difference between what you feel and what the world really is.'

I got excited thinking about science practicals. 'That's so true!'

The law student couldn't have looked more supercilious. He was still listening in, his thin face and cigar wreathing around in the backround behind Murphy's red velvet seat.

Murphy went on: 'And human beings are really absurd because they look for meaning in things and things have no fucking meaning at all.'

I gulped down a huge drink of cider, trying to be like Murphy. The room swam around me for a few seconds.

'Take possessions for instance, it's really stupid,' Murphy said.

I agreed, thinking about my father and how he cried when he had to sell his land: *oh god where did you come from that you can't understand land?* The way he fingered his bank statements.

'Land is stupid.' I had lots of intelligent thoughts in my head but I couldn't get them out. Murphy didn't seem to mind.

'Especially if you don't have it,' Murphy guffawed, and I felt ashamed of the fact that my father had land. 'But seriously, it's all absurd like. It's like suicide. That's your department.' He gave me a nudge. I could see he was still impressed with my brick-throwing.

Murphy finished his pint urgently. Cords stood out on his neck and made me feel uncomfortable. I covered my own neck protectively. He stood up, swung his tool-box, and winked at Carl. Fierce obvious. 'Oh, I wanted to know more about existentialism.' I couldn't bear them to think that I was pleased to get Carl on my own. Murphy winked at Carl again and walked out, every eye in the bar following him.

'What kind of a trade has he, anyway?' I asked Carl.

'The fuck knows,' Carl said.

We were sitting there. Murphy had been discreet, leaving us alone. We were both thinking this, I knew it. Carl put his legs up on the chair. I loved his thin legs.

'Skinhead!' said a voice. 'Take your filthy boots down!' The supercilious law student peered over Carl's seat.

'I fucking won't!' said Carl.

A rugby player's head appeared. 'Move those fucking legs, boy.'

My heart bumped against my ribs. The biggest head I'd ever seen. I knew that he was a friend of the law student. They'd beat up Carl.

'Put them down,' I said.

'I fucking won't.' Carl's face was going red.

Carl couldn't back down so I put a hand up to my head and gave a scream to divert them. Carl tried to catch my head in his hands, but I began to twist it from side to side. I thrashed a bit, but not too much because I didn't want to squash the safety pins down the sides of my jeans.

Another head, a girl's head this time, came over the red velvet seat. 'Call an ambulance!'

'Yes, it could be an overdose,' said the supercilious law student.

I thought that I saw someone going for the phone and the barman was coming out from behind the counter. I ran like mad through the lounge, tearing at the collar of my shirt.

When we got outside, we ran into into wasteland across from the pub in case they sent an ambulance after us. It was safe to laugh now. The wind was cutting into Carl's thin black T-shirt but he didn't seem to notice. And he could run effortlessly with those long thin legs of his.

'Hey, stop, you know I can't run like that!' I said.

Carl stopped and put his arms around me. I could feel his brilliant thin body and his heart pumping. His lips were covered with salt.

The kiss didn't take very long. Carl was out of breath. I put the moaning couples in the Arc firmly out of my mind.

'I want to be an existentialist,' I said, with wild abandon.

'I can't go out with you!'

'Oh why not?' I hated the clingy way I was talking, but he had given me a shock. 'I don't take up too much time.'

'I can't take the risk, there's only a few weeks left.' Carl took my hand. 'Don't be mad, we can go out in London.'

'That's if I'm still available,' I said, really mad, wiping his salt off my lips. 'I might have topped myself with a brick by then.'

Carl threw a brick through a window on his way home. Strangled shouts came from inside the house. As we ran, the perspiration hung in silver clusters on his eyelashes. I didn't sweat but my chest was cut up from the terrible exertion.

Carl said that he wasn't going to go out with someone who was going to tell him what to do. If he wanted to pursue violence he fucking would.

· *Eleven* ·

Ger wasn't really a diabolical agent. I could see that as soon as I returned to daylight. But we never went back to Pierce's flat. Ger was as miserable as can be. I longed to tell her to give him up except I didn't dare.

Even though the knocking in the kitchen stopped, we were still scared. It became a routine, always going upstairs early together, not looking at the stained mirrors in the bedroom, keeping the curtains open so that the dawn woke us and we were exhausted for hours before we got up. Bird-calls like little red-hot hammers against our aching heads.

It wasn't long either before I realized that Ger didn't have acute alcoholic gastritus.

She was relieved when I asked her one grey morning as she staggered back from the bathroom, looking poisoned.

'That's why I'm going to London.'

'But will it be in time?'

'Just over three months, maybe a bit over.'

We had discussed abortions before. Decided they were the right thing to do. How else could we be liberated? Yet I hadn't thought it would really happen to either of us. I don't think that Ger had either.

'Are you sure?'
'Of course I'm sure!'

I knew nothing of course, but I felt that I should have pressed her more. Or Pierce should have.

'What does *he* think?'

'Myra's nerves are bad,' was the answer from Ger and she didn't sound a bit convinced or sympathetic. 'It's over anyway, he's an eedjit. I burn with shame every time I think of him.'

'Ah, he's not bad, just a bit old.'

'He's fucking ancient! Weak as water. Proud then on top of it. Pride! You never saw the likes of it!'

Where was Ger going to get the money for it? She refused to ask Pierce. Then she decided to do it herself. The knocking in the kitchen came straight back. Instead of taking the warning, she went right ahead with her inexorable carry on. Said that it was I that was drawing the spirits with my banshee moans and wringing hands.

Just because I wouldn't jump on her stomach with my boots on or jump on her stomach with bare feet. I sat gingerly on her stomach twice when she went on her knees and begged me. I loaned her three pounds towards the bottle of gin but she only vomited it straight up and got red marks on her legs from the boiling-hot bath.

What was the point of wasting good money when you could do it yourself? she wanted to know. She said that I was like one of those hypocrites who're happy to eat a chicken but wouldn't dream of wringing its neck themselves.

'Jesus, I *am* one of those hypocrites!' I shouted. 'I know I know nothing about killing chickens. I wouldn't want to make it suffer more because I'm useless.'

'There's nobody killing anything here.' Ger kept changing her tack. 'I'm just trying to bring my periods on.'

Then Ger got hold of a knitting needle from the crafts section of Matthews and I really went berserk. I tried to wrest it from her when we got home, but she said that she'd have the eye out of my head and pointed it straight at my left pupil.

'Why didn't you use contraception?' I asked her, backing away like the selfish coward I was.

'I used the safe period.'

'There's no such thing,' I said, amazed that even I knew more than Ger, and I wouldn't be able to have sex to save my life.

'Pierce said that Myra always swore by ten days before and ten days after your period.'

'But Myra couldn't have children anyway!'

'And do you not think that I haven't worked that out for myself since!'

I covered my eyes at the sight of her. Long black hair awry, stalking along the corridor to the bathroom in her long purple dress like someone from the House of Usher.

At first there was a huge thud, then the scream when it came was more of a whimper. Ger limped out of the bathroom looking cowed.

'Well?' I asked, nearly hoping she'd got it over and done with.

'I think I've hurt my ankle.'

'How did you manage that!'

'Oh, I couldn't do it in the end. So I decided to stand on the bathroom chair and jump violently.'

She'd always been so sensible, refusing to go out

with anyone in case it interfered with her studies. I wondered if Pierce wasn't a kind of Bluebeard who drove women mad instead of killing them. How many more mad women had he got locked away in mental institutions all over the country?

I went with Ger to the college doctor and he gave her a prescription for Valium and bandaged her ankle. He wasn't very good at bandages. Ger complained that it gave her no support and it unwound itself slowly as we walked down the road to the pharmacist.

The woman in the pharmacy was tut-tutting as she made up the prescription. She told Ger to get out of her long dress and do a bit of exercise. She told me to take any idea I had of stealing drugs right out of my mind, because she had a mirror in the back where she made up the prescriptions and an alarm button that rang straight away in the Bridewell Garda Station.

The insults didn't stop but we were too tired to answer back. I tried to adjust the chair I was sitting on and discovered that it was screwed to the ground. I nearly amputated my hand. Luckily the chair wasn't in the line of vision of the mirror at the back or she'd have had to prove that her alarm button *was* connected to the Bridewell.

I was holding my wrist as we hailed a taxi outside the shop. The taximan wanted to know if we'd been in a scrap, savage with us because we only wanted to go three hundred yards to our flat.

· Twelve ·

Ger was considering getting a bank loan when I left to get the number eight into town. We'd written out a big shopping list for things like eggs and brown bread and yoghurt. Maybe if we were healthier we'd stop hearing the noises.

There was a woman with a load of children at the bus-stop. She wasn't that old, about twenty-eight. I had a guilt problem when I saw mothers. I didn't know where to look. And it was half embarrassing too, the children so milky. Like nakedness of some sort.

We waited ages for the bus. A fine misty rain was falling. I gave the mother sympathetic looks and smiled at the children. Of course one smile was no good. They wanted you to keep at it. Hiding round the bus-stop, peeping behind their fingers, all that sort of stuff. If I wasn't careful they were going to get me playing with them.

I looked distant then, pretended not to see their insistent stares, hating myself the whole time. There was an older child behind wearing brown boots that were either fierce trendy or old-fashioned but I couldn't see his face.

The bus swayed up, big and unwieldy. Some fool of a man in a blue suit with biscuit-coloured sheepskin gloves was trying to buy a ticket with a twenty-pound note, holding us all up outside in the rain. The mother was trying to fold up her pushchair.

'I'll lift her in to you,' I said, picking up the toddler, when at last someone gave twenty pence to the man with the twenty-pound note so that we could all start getting on.

I felt so chivalrous helping the woman that I began passing all her children up the steps. Some of them were quite heavy and I wasn't sure if the older ones wanted to be lifted because they started to wriggle. I decided to be firm and lifted them all up, even the biggish one with the brown boots and what I could now see was a black balaclava over its head.

It was a bit of a struggle, but I flung it in ahead of me and clambered up the steps shaking the rain off my head. That's when I saw that it wasn't a child at all. Just a very small man who was now screaming at me in a funny voice. A voice like a thirty-three record played on forty-five.

'Ya saucy pup, ya young blackguard! Ya scut of the highest order.'

I was mortified. It was a desperate thing to do. Picking up a dwarf, slinging him on to the bus! Surely no one could believe that I'd do it deliberately? I was surprised the way the bus driver was allowing him to go on.

I sat down in confusion, right opposite the little man who was swinging his legs furiously, blowing his cheeks in and out. The mother and children had gone upstairs, without a backward glance or a word of thanks.

He snatched off his balaclava and I had to sit there with everyone looking at me. He was bald-headed, scowling, fifty at least. A small version of my father.

'Ya lighting hoor, ya interferin jade, ya septic oinseach, ya black Protestant!' He shouted on and on.

I thought someone might stand up for me, or at least tell him to shut up after I whispered sorry a couple of times, but they all stayed quiet. The man with the twenty-pound note had a faint smile which he was trying to hide with his biscuity gloves. Two young boys were craning forward shamelessly to get a better look at my face and a thin grey widowy woman kept saying 'disgraceful' under her breath.

I stood up and rang the bell to get off. The rain was teeming now, waterfalls gushing down the window panes. I didn't even know where we were or where I was getting off.

'That's right, run away when you've had enough of your blackguarding. You'll be old some day. See if you like being carted around then. Like a sack of spuds. Oh you thought you were funny but do you see anyone laughing?'

The man with the twenty-pound note stopped smiling, everyone looked straight ahead. It galled me. Why should I think that I was wrong just because the rest of the world was a crowd of cowards! I swayed right over to where he sat with his brown boots dangling two feet above the floor. 'One more word out of you and I'll lay you out.' His brown boots rose and went straight out as he put his hands over his head and ducked. He nearly got me in the stomach and he wasn't even trying..

'Oh mother of divine Jesus,' said the widow. The two young boys started giggling and I was afraid that the man with the sheepskin gloves would get up to apprehend me.

'Now, fuck off home to Snow White!' I shouted and sprang out as the doors swished open.

I had about two minutes of dark glory, flames of triumph that burned along my limbs.

The flames died down very quick when I started feeling bad. Taking advantage of his size, *flying in the face of the Almighty.*

Safely on the pavement, I looked around, hardly able to see with the weight of raindrops that were hanging off my eyelashes. I realized that the bus had only gone a few yards. Even taking account of the heavy traffic, we must have been on the bus only a few minutes.

I couldn't help thinking that he had the face of a rat. That rat in the gutter who roared PASSPORT! PASSPORT! in *The Steadfast Tin Soldier.* STOP! STOP! YOU HAVEN'T PAID YOUR TOLL!

I walked along the pavement feeling damned. *You'll have no luck for it!* You were supposed to be kind to your parents and unfortunates. Because. *You'll be old some day.*

· *Thirteen* ·

Pierce called round to see Ger. I came in at the end. Ger looked as if she'd been crying and Pierce looked relieved when he saw me. I was sorry to be the agent of his relief.

'Wouldn't you think Fred and the lads would have investigated those noises in the kitchen when it was in their power to do so? You're so vague it's hard to know whether it's just nerves with the two of you.'

Ger flinched when Pierce mentioned nerves. I wished that I could say something to cut him. I could see what Ger meant about pride though. He walked so tall going out the door he hit his head off the lintel. And kept going, even when the pain must have been killing him.

I should have stayed with Ger but Carl had asked me to call round. Ger kept saying she was fine and I wanted to get away from the flat. Fred hadn't come up with the physics notes that he'd promised. I said nothing about it, I had my pride. But it rankled every time I saw him.

Carl and Tom were living on packet soup, bread and coffee. Tom took a ten-minute break every two hours to smoke a cigarette and Carl lay on the floor with his legs against the wall. Tom spoke about food, three-inch steaks, his mother's Irish stew. It drove Carl mad, he was starving. Tom's mother was supposed to be calling round.

The whole place was covered in dust and the kitchen stank. A pile of dirty saucepans was stacked against the wall and a thin yellow line of melted butter drizzled across the kitchen table. The sitting room was scattered with empty tin-foil cartons from the Happy Gardens Chinese Restaurant.

'She's bringing food, I'll get her to clear up as well.'

'You must be joking! I wouldn't ask my worst enemy to clear up this room.' Carl put his hand up, shading his eyes from the sight of it.

'She'd only love to do it.'

'Why?' Carl and I spoke together.

'She just would.'

'Is she a masochist or what?' Carl asked.

'She likes doing things for me.'

'What food is she bringing?'

'Oh probably steaks, lamb chops, maybe a chicken and a big bag of potatoes.'

Tom put out his cigarette and was lying on the floor with his legs in the air, studying a circuit diagram. 'I think there's a mistake here, they should have put a resistor along the bottom.'

Carl stared at the wall for a minute. I wondered if I should go away. I couldn't offer to clean up because I was a woman.

Ger said that we had to be careful about things like that. We were role models for the younger women coming behind us. I thought tenderly about the ghostly younger women behind me. They weren't

93

ghostly to Ger, she was thinking about her younger sisters.

Carl cleared all the Happy Gardens cartons into plastic bags and put them outside the back door. He filled the kitchen sink with hot soapy water and washed all the dirty dishes. I found something like a tea towel and began drying up.

As long as I did less than they did.

Tom dried the dishes as well and wiped the kitchen table. He even scrubbed the yellow butter drizzle off the formica. It took him about ten minutes, puffing and hissing through his teeth.

'Better not frighten her off with too much dirt.' He rubbed at a black footprint he'd suddenly seen on the floor.

She didn't arrive until half two. Carl said that he had a hole in his stomach thinking about lamb chops and roast chicken.

She was very attractive and young-looking in a gypsy way. She had a slim yet sturdy body with dark brown hair falling in untidy layers down to her shoulders. Her eyes and her skin were brown too and she wore jeans. She kissed Tom really hard on the lips and he didn't seem to mind.

'And you're Carl.' She gripped Carl's hand tightly in her small brown one. She shook my hand too. I liked the feel of her hand, hot, dry and smooth. She carried an empty-looking brown suede shoulder-bag and nothing else.

Carl stared at it and then noticed her looking at him. 'Do you want a cup of coffee?'

'Okay.' She didn't seem pushed about anything.

Carl and I went down to the kitchen. Carl said that he was shaking with the hunger. He wished that he'd made up some minestrone soup from the packet earlier. Tom had drunk a whole packet of cream of celery, but Carl didn't like cream of celery and besides he'd been saving himself for the lamb chops.

We could hear laughter coming from the sitting room, Tom and his mother laughing at some joke.

'Maybe Tom was having me on. Is that what they're laughing at?'

'Don't be stupid,' I said, feeling superior. Annoyed too. Why was he always bothering about what older women thought?

He banged on the kettle and put a match to the gas flame. Rummaging in the bread bin, he found a heel of bread and heaped it with butter. In the cupboard he found an almost empty jar of raspberry jam, and scraped a thin pink film across the butter. Pushing half of it into his mouth, he began to chew.

The front door slammed. Footsteps came towards the kitchen. It was Tom and his mother. Tom was swinging two plastic bags. They must have gone to her car to get them.

'I didn't hear you go out,' Carl said and sat down, still looking weak.

A bag of jam doughnuts, a bottle of wine and that was all.

'Lovely,' I said, but I was very disappointed for Carl.

'Don't bother with the coffee,' Tom's mother said and dolloped a load of red wine into a mug. She didn't need to be told that there weren't any glasses.

'Help yourself.' She waved at the bag of jam doughnuts. She didn't take one herself though. Opening her limp suede bag, she took out a packet of Silk Cut and a silver lighter.

Carl was still trying to finish his crust of bread with jam and butter.

'Take no notice of me,' she said, waving the smoke

away from her face with her brown hand. I thought that she got prettier the more I looked at her. I had a nagging feeling that Carl thought so too.

'Oh, no!' she said suddenly and put her hands up to the sides of her head. 'The lamb chops!'

Carl looked at her. Two faint blotches appeared over his cheekbones, but I didn't think that she'd notice. She didn't know him as well as I did.

'I forgot all the meat, the lamb chops, steak and I even had a bit of salmon. Took them out of the deep freeze and left them on the kitchen table. Well, shit!'

'It doesn't matter in the slightest, Josie,' Tom said straight away. Too quickly, I thought.

Tom wasn't talking as much as usual and he had his eyes fixed on the bottle of red wine. Josie kept refilling her mug and Tom kept grabbing it and refilling his mug. He didn't even drink wine usually, but he was tearing into this bottle. Like there was a race on.

His mother won. She got the last glass, and it was only then, after putting out her cigarette, that she relaxed and ate a doughnut. She didn't seem to give a damn, licked the jam from her fingers, lit another cigarette and threw her head back to blow the smoke towards the ceiling.

Tom seemed annoyed. 'I'll get you some tissues,' he said and stomped off to the bathroom.

We could hear him banging around. I didn't know where he was going to find tissues as they never had any.

Tom came back with a roll of toilet paper and banged it down on the table.

'Did you get the tan in France?' Carl asked politely.

'We were there for Easter, did Tom tell you?' Her speech was slightly slurred. Just slightly, like when you can't get a radio station exactly.

'No, he didn't. What part of France?'

'The Dordogne, we always go there. Ever since Tom was little. His French is good. Have you heard him?'

Tom slouched sulkily. 'For fuck's sake, Josie, don't go on about it. Carl doesn't want to hear all this crap.'

I was amazed at his language. I could see Carl was annoyed too because he got an obvious fit of coughing.

Josie was funny the way she ignored Tom. You'd never think that he'd just been raging at her. She put her hand on Tom's head and felt his short haircut. He didn't stop her and you could see that he half liked it.

'Why don't we go for a sandwich somewhere? You've been waiting for me to come with all this meat. And I feel so bad I must buy you something. Carl, I can't bear to see you gnawing. Crusts and doughnuts won't take you far. You too, Maeve. You're very pale-looking.'

'That's make-up,' Tom said.

'It's not make-up. I don't wear any on my face.' I was raging.

'White skin is nice too.' Josie beamed at us. As if we had a complex about not having a tan and needed to be reassured.

'No, I really must bring you both for lunch. Is there a pub nearby?'

'Here we go,' muttered Tom under his breath.

Josie turned to Carl. '*You'll* tell me, won't you? Where's your local? Would they do you a ham sandwich?'

'Well, there's Curtains,' Carl suggested, looking doubtful. We never went to pubs for food. We'd hardly enough money for drink.

Josie stood up and folded the bag of doughnuts closed. 'Put them in the fridge for later.'

Tom swung up from his chair. I expected him to do something violent, but he just put the doughnuts in the fridge and took a Silk Cut from Josie's packet. I'd never seen him smoking before. He was wearing a military-style pale-blue shirt. It was long and thin and clung to his body.

Did Tom really wear his father's clothes? Ger thought that he was stealing them all from the dramatic society.

'Don't forget to lock that back door before we leave,' Josie ordered Tom as she followed Carl out of the kitchen.

'Right.'

Tom's unlit cigarette bobbed furiously between his lips as he shot the bolt home. It was very tense in the yellow Volkswagon. I could hear Carl's stomach rumbling.

· *Fourteen* ·

When we arrived at Curtains, Ger was there. Sitting by herself. I could see Tom looking at her strapped ankle but I didn't explain it. It was always better to say nothing, Ger said.

Tom was with Josie at the bar ordering the drinks. Josie was trying to talk Myra into making a sandwich.

'No, no, I've no ham, there's no point in asking me for what I haven't got.'

'Have you got tomatoes or even eggs?'

'Look here, I'm on my own. Am I going to go upstairs now boiling eggs? Am I?'

'Sardines?'

'No.' Myra gave Josie a small smile. 'I can make you a cheese, but it's that cat stuff.'

'Calvita?'

'No, worse again, it's those Easi Slices.'

'Give us anything,' Josie said. 'We're starving.'

'I'm okay,' I said.

'Don't be stupid, you can't live on chocolate. No wonder you've got those dark circles under your eyes,' Josie said.

I didn't think that I'd any circles under my eyes and besides I didn't see what was so healthy about Easi Slices.

'I'm telling you they wreck themselves,' Myra agreed. 'Staying up all night, drinking black coffee and studying.'

Completely untrue in my case. Even Ger had early nights when she was studying. I went over to Ger's table, irked. Just because Josie and Myra were ancient they thought that they could make remarks. If you gave them half a chance, they'd be managing us.

Ger asked me about Josie. 'Has Tom got an older woman?'

'I'm telling you it's his mother.'

'She's fierce attractive.'

'And bossy,' I said.

'Her hair is brilliant, the way it's so untidy. Look, she's got a pint of Guinness.' Ger smoked dreamily.

I pushed three Rolos into my mouth together and squinted at Josie. I wished that I could drink Guinness. It looked so beautiful, the dark curved column, the cream drawn to the top, but it tasted cat.

'Maeve, for god's sake, she's not blind.' Ger gave me a little push and I realised that I'd been staring at Josie.

'Sorry, sorry.' I wrenched my eyes away and began reading a beer-mat. It looked really obvious, but Josie didn't seem to notice as she came over and sat down with us.

She wasn't drunk, but there was something wrong with her walk, that slight slurring of her speech. Like as if she just needed one more drink to be flaming. I thought that I'd try to be nice for Tom's sake. We didn't mind if she got drunk, but he did.

His body was stiff and every time the glass went to his mother's lips, he took an even bigger drink himself.

'Are you a punkette?' Josie asked me. It was kind of

touching the way that Josie was so pleased with herself for knowing the right word.

I couldn't help feeling pleased either. 'I was thinking about dying my hair navy when I go to London.'

'Navy blue,' said Josie and scooped a bit of Guinness head from the side of her glass with her brown paw. You couldn't figure out whether she thought that it was a good idea or not, but I was glad that she didn't give her opinion this time.

Tom stood up violently. I thought that he was going to take the glass off Josie. Draining his drink, he announced that he was going to get another round.

'It's my turn,' Carl said.

'What are you having?' Tom spoke heavily.

'You know we never go into rounds.' I put my hand over the top of my glass.

'Jesus, I'm not going to insist,' Tom said, looking at my hand contemptuously.

Josie opened her suede bag and took out a soft green leather wallet. 'Take this fiver, Tom, and get drinks for us all.'

Ger and I protested only a little bit. Josie kept smiling, crinkling tiny brown lines around her eyes.

Myra came out bearing the cheese sandwich on a black and gold lacquered tray. She was still wearing her white coat and she had a pair of thick black socks on over her tights.

'It's freezing, I'm telling you.' She put the sandwiches on the table. 'No charge now, that's a little present from me.'

Everyone looked at the sandwiches. They didn't look right.

'I toasted them specially in the microwave.' The bread was snow-white and orange pools of melted cheese dripped down the sides. It didn't look a bit toasted.

Josey put her hand gently on it and her thumb sunk into the bread, leaving a deep impression. 'It's a bit soft, isn't it?'

'Oh, you have to leave it a few minutes to coagulate, it'll be lovely and chewy in a few minutes, you'll see.' Myra walked back to the counter. I thought that her hair was getting greyer. No wonder Pierce was after Ger.

'Myra's a bit weird,' I explained to Josie.

'I think she's a gas case,' Josie said, feeling her sandwich again. 'I thinking it's getting there, it's rubbering up.' She took another drink of Guinness.

Tom took a huge quaff from his drink as soon as he saw Josie's lips reaching the glass. He didn't take his eyes from her the whole time he was drinking. The level of his pint sank about two and a half inches.

'I think Myra is mad,' I continued, feeling that I had to explain things to Josie. In case Josie ever found out about Ger and judged her too harshly.

I leaned over and whispered to Josie, 'I think it's hard on Pierce.'

I saw Ger staring at me and I stopped.

Josie only laughed. 'She sounds like me. Tom's father has a desperate time coping with *my* nerves. Doesn't he, Tom?'

Tom shrugged. His face looked pale and out of focus. He was the one who was getting drunker. Josie seemed to stay the same.

'Myra's right, this sandwich is very chewy,' she said, tugging at it with her teeth.

'Where's Pierce?' I asked Ger.

'How should I know?' Ger looked cross and embarrassed.

102

I wanted to talk to Carl but he was doodling on the back of a beer mat and I could hardly ask what's that when it was just a scribble. Tom and Ger were like two bears and Carl began eating the sandwiches.

Then Fred arrived and sat down. Still no one spoke. I thought about those physics notes. I would give him five minutes to mention them.

'I've just heard about the most fantastic seance someone had up on Richmond Hill.'

'Do you expect Maeve and Ger to go to a seance ever again?' Carl was disgusted.

'They're going to do the exact same thing again on Saturday night if anyone's interested,' Fred went on, ignoring Carl.

'Did you say seance?' Josie shook her hair out of her eyes.

'Yes, I did.' Fred stared at Josie admiringly. That annoyed me.

'Do I know you?' Fred went into his how-do-you-do voice.

'I'm Josie.' She put out her hand. 'Tom's mother.'

'Well, Tom, you ah well . . .' Fred exaggerated how he was stuck for words.

'Don't talk to me about seances,' Josie butted in.

'You've had some too?' This was interesting. I opened a packet of Mintolas. Carl yanked on his sandwich. I wondered if Fred might inspire Carl to make a go for me before the exams. If he did I'd brush him off light-heartedly.

'My grandfather was a rational man,' announced Josie, pushing the rest of her orange and white sandwich to Carl.

'Where are you leading us?' Fred gave a little shiver.

'My Aunt Lizzy came home from America to die.

She was an early feminist, but she got something fatal, had to leave her work in America.'

'Feminist!' Tom snorted. 'Wasn't she a servant-girl? Haven't you got a picture of her in her frilly cap and the works?'

'Yes, the photograph taken by her employer, the great suffragette.'

I wanted to ask who the Great Suffragette was but Josie went on straight away.

'Lizzy was highly intelligent. All my side of the family were.'

Tom gave Josie a look.

'What's the point of false modesty? Lizzy came back from New York with a suitcase of beautiful clothes, dark silk dresses, soft leather button boots. A silver fur cape. I'd love to know what became of it. Auntie Agnes was deadly for stealing of course. It wasn't TB. I think it was Lizzy's heart. It took about a year and she used to walk around the village with a big black dog.'

My throat went dry when I heard 'black dog'. I caught Ger's eye. 'Was it a smooth-haired terrier?' I asked.

'How would I know what kind of a dog it was? They didn't photograph it! But it was definitely *big*. A big black dog. A wolfhound maybe!'

'Wolfhounds are grey,' Tom interrupted.

'Are they? Oh well, it wasn't a wolfhound then. The crowds at Mass would part when she arrived. She was tall, carried herself well. Of course those other fools of servant-girls came back from America like clowns, their faces plastered with rouge. Gaudy yellow dresses.' Josie's eyes were misty, as if she'd been there.

'So what happened?' Carl asked.

'How do you mean what happened? She died of course.'

'And what about your grandfather?'

'I was getting to that bit. My grandfather was a rational man.'

'Rational, oh yes, rational,' Tom muttered.

'Will you stop,' Ger hissed, 'I want to hear the story.'

'Thank you,' said Josie. 'The night she was buried, the other two daughters, that's Hannah Maria and Kathleen,' she added, looking at Tom who was looking deep into his pint, 'were asleep in bed and the knocking started in the downstairs bedroom where she'd died and been laid out.' Josie gave three sharp knocks on the formica table. I jumped. 'Then the howling started. Supernatural. Roaring and the wind, the two daughters ran into their father's bedroom.'

'Where was their mother?'

'I can't remember anything about her, she must have been dead already.'

'Already, dead already, who gives a shit?' Tom said.

'Well they're all dead now,' Josie said. 'My grandfather caught the two of them by the hand and led them down the stairs. He believed, you see, that there was an explanation for everything. And there was.'

Josie lit another cigarette, flourishing her lighter. 'The window was open to air the room and the wind had caught hold of the handle of the blind. It was knocking, knocking, knocking, on the window-pane.' Knock, knock, knock went Josie's small brown hand on the table.

'And on the empty bed with the covers thrown back was the dog going round and round, crying his heart out. Only for my grandfather making them investigate they'd have thought it was a ghost, you see. Of course the poor old dog was put down.'

Josie was acting as if she'd reassured us all with her rational grandfather, but the sadness of it! The lonely dying woman and her faithful companion. I hoped that she came back to haunt the bastard who got the dog put down. I decided to try to be nice to that black dog if I ever saw him again. Who was to say that he wasn't carrying a torch for some brave dead person?

Josie got up and kissed Tom on the cheek and he patted her small back in its pale-blue jumper. She went over to the bar door and waved when she got it opened. Her legs weaved a small bit.

· Fifteen ·

The door had hardly closed behind Josie when Best and Jimmy Barry came swaggering in. I couldn't understand it, you could see that they didn't like each other really. Ger said that was *boys*. *Boys* had no integrity. *Boys* would do anything to impress each other. Ger had taken to calling any man younger than Pierce *a boy*. I don't know what she was trying to prove. I didn't care what she called them, no way would I ever go near someone as old as Pierce.

'Ever fall in love with someone you shouldn't've?' Jimmy Barry said to Ger and she jumped a mile.

She told him to fuck off.

'That's the Buzzcocks,' he said, smirking.

I thought he was horrible making sly insinuations about Pierce, but then I thought he could have been referring to himself. It was hard to know with Jimmy Barry, his face was a permanent lemon.

Ger wasn't having any of it anyway, she was rolling a cigarette for Tom. If it was an attempt to sober him up, it didn't work. About a half an hour after Josie left, Tom suddenly slid to the floor. He sat for a moment with his head sunk on his chest, then his body relaxed flat as his head went under the chair.

Myra rushed out from behind the counter, her white

coat swinging. 'I'll never forgive myself.' She knelt beside him and opened the buttons of his shirt.

Jimmy Barry looked annoyed but Best looked relieved. Best's bandaged foot was up on a chair. He thought he was on holidays from wrecky but Jimmy Barry said that now was the time to press on with the work that he'd started.

'You're not going to let a scratch on your leg stop you?' Jimmy Barry said and stepped over Tom's body. 'Come on, Best, we've got things to do.'

Myra gave him a bad look. 'Is that a way to treat your friend?'

'He's only langers, for fuck's sake,' Jimmy Barry said. 'Come on, Best.' Best limped after Jimmy Barry.

'He doesn't need air, he's just drunk,' Fred said.

'I should have known, I should have known,' Myra said.

'Well, why did you keep serving him?' Fred asked, officiously.

'Don't be such a pain, how was she to know that he was going to collapse after five pints? Normally he can drink ten before he falls,' Carl snapped.

'I should have known, it's true.' Myra shrugged her coat off and released her batwing sleeves. 'He was getting chasers every time he came up with an order. I knew he was nervous because his Mum was drinking with you. I didn't like to stop the poor creature. I wouldn't mind but she is well able to hold her drink.'

I looked at Carl. 'You'll have to take him home now.'

I wished that I hadn't ignored Carl, trying to appear preoccupied and interesting.

'Yes,' Carl said, grimly.

'How will you manage?'

'We'll give you a hand,' Myra said, and put her

hands over her eyes again to show how sorry she was. 'Send a strong man!' we heard her shout when she called for the taxi. She pressed a fiver into Carl's hand.

The door opened again and that crowd of girls from my science practicals arrived. Claire was with them and she sat down with us for a minute, laughing into her Britvic orange.

'You just missed Best,' Fred said.

'I wasn't looking for him.' Claire was serious. 'Where are those notes you promised me?'

'Nine o'clock tomorrow morning, come to the physics department,' Fred said, avoiding my eye.

'He promised me notes too,' I said to Claire as soon as I got a moment.

Claire exploded into laughter and I sat there feeling humiliated, waiting for the worst of her attack to subside. When she got her breath back, she said there was no problem. We could share or photocopy them.

'I'm going to fail anyway,' I said.

'Claire was only looking for Best,' Ger said after Claire left, her clean denim figure going off purposefully.

'Oh for god's sake, why should we judge?' I said.

'You mean I shouldn't be judging?' Ger said. 'Because of Pierce? Is that what you're getting at?'

It wasn't what I meant. I had felt bad for being suspicious of Claire chasing the physics notes, but I didn't say this to Ger. I looked at Myra filling a pint behind the counter. 'But don't you feel bad?'

'I do, it's just that I can't help it and anyway she's as mad as a hatter. It's not fair on Pierce. She knocks back bottles of pills.'

Myra flung out her arms again, talking to a customer.

'Look at that!' Ger exclaimed. 'Does that look like a sane woman to you?'

'Maybe she's giving directions,' I offered.

'That's part of it, you know.'

'What?'

'Pierce says that she can't stop giving directions. Like she's some kind of oracle for travellers. She spends evenings studying maps of Cork.'

'It must be hard on him,' I said, imagining Pierce with his new strained face sitting on the sofa, while Myra rolled and unrolled maps. The rattling noise.

'He had to call the doctor at two in the morning.'

'Jesus!'

'She got really drunk, started ringing up people, telling them that Pierce was chasing her around the bar with a gun.'

I couldn't stop looking at Myra.

'Stop staring!' Ger said. 'She'll see you!'

I looked into my glass for a moment and then sneaked another look. The bar was empty.

'Where is she?' Her sudden disappearance seemed ominous.

'Oh she's probably in the back, dropping tablets. Come on! I want to check my eyeliner.'

I leaned my back against the washbasin. Ger stood in front of the mirror, smoking gloomily, her eyes fixed on her own reflection. 'Look at my face, it's all puffy. You'd know I was pregnant.'

'It isn't a bit! Pierce doesn't have a gun?'

'He does, but he was only messing!'

'You mean he did chase her round the bar?'

'No, no, no! He just made some joke, that's all.'

'What kind of a joke?'

'Oh, I don't know! Maybe, "If you don't shut up, I'll shoot you!" '

'That's not much of a joke! My god, if someone said that to me, I'd throw myself out the window!'

'You're as bad!'

'I'm not! And Pierce's eyes can look really violent sometimes, you know when he bulges them at you!'

'No, I don't actually, Maeve.'

I thought about Myra, throwing her arms out, poring over maps. 'I suppose it must be hard. She's definitely weird! That sandwich she made for Josie.'

'Well, this is it.' Ger heaved a thick plume of smoke from her mouth and looked consoled. 'Let's get a bottle of cider to take home!' She put her cigarette out.

Ger went into one toilet and I went into another one. The door opened, I could hear someone running the water. I tried to think of something nice to say to Ger.

'You know it's like Jane Eyre and mad Mrs Rochester!'

Ger didn't answer. The running water stopped.

'You're Jane Eyre,' I tried again, and the outer door banged shut. There was still no answer from Ger, only a wrenching sound as she came out of the other toilet.

I came out and Ger was standing in front of the hand-drier.

'Do you realise,' – Ger hit the hand-drier with her fist – 'that Myra is the only other woman in the bar tonight?'

The hand-drier roared into action as I covered my mouth with my hand. 'But she wouldn't guess!'

'She wouldn't half.' Ger leaned over the hand-drier.

'Do you feel sick?' I asked.

'Sick at heart,' Ger said as the door flew open and Myra stuck her head in.

'Well, how's Jane Eyre?' Myra asked sarcastically, fumes of brandy floating across the poky room.

Ger didn't even try to speak.

'Do you know anything about Jean Rhys?'

Ger flinched when Myra said Jean Rhys! I wondered if she was an old girlfriend of Pierce's.

'And for the benefit of the half-educated,' Myra flung at me, 'Jean Rhys wrote a book about the other Mrs Rochester, the one who was supposed to be mad!' She looked again at Ger. 'Giving *her* side of the story.'

Ger stood, her face crimson, a cigarette burning into her fingers. She didn't speak.

'It's called *Wide Sargasso Sea*!' Myra said to me. 'Write that down, you might like to read it.' She banged the door out and the smell of brandy went with her.

Ger hit the hand-drier again and again, blowing hot air over her red face.

· *Sixteen* ·

Dominic from my zoology class saw me colouring in a picture of the cell in the reading rooms and laughed at me. 'You know how to waste time! We'll never get asked that!'

I had avoided Fred since he'd told Claire she could have the physics notes. Claire wanted to share them, but I avoided her too. I got grinds from someone else from the physics department. He kept telling me that all I had to do was to keep my head in the exam. Why did they say that? You were either keeping your head or you couldn't. And if you needed them to tell you in the first place then you definitely couldn't. It was the kind of stupid thing that people always went on with. Like telling you to 'relax' and 'stop worrying' and 'put up with things'.

I wished that I was like Ger. Ger who was pregnant and disappointed yet threw herself into the books even more. Ger stared at her books and wrote loads of notes, her black hair pouring over her shoulders, her pink mouth in the straightest line. I felt like putting my ruler against it, to confirm its straightness and measure the length of it. Maybe work out the angles it formed with the sides of her nose.

I was doing science because my father said an arts

degree was useless, that I'd never get a job. But Ger had high hopes and I knew that I'd never get a science job anyway. I wouldn't be much good in a lab. I was afraid of holding test tubes and I couldn't use a pipette to save my life. I always let go the stuff I was sucking up. I didn't trust myself not to swallow it.

Or what if it was something like physics practicals, balancing weights and pendulums and working out weird answers? What kind of a job was that? How could I possibly teach it? Once we had to rig up a load of red and black electrical leads, connect them with resistors and ammeters and all that kind of stuff. When you got all the connections right an electric bulb lit up on a board.

A couple of people got it straight away. The rest of us made encouraging faces at each other as we plugged and unplugged hundreds of black and red leads. The afternoon wore on and there were fewer and fewer encouraging faces, as more and more electric light bulbs lit up around the benches. My bulb never lit up.

I was vindicated when the cell came up on my zoology paper. I looked for Dominic to point this out to him but he wasn't around. Otherwise the exams were fearful. A pain in my gut from looking at the clock, the way the second hand swung around when I was trying to puzzle out the physics problems. 'Puzzle' makes it sound like I was calm, like I was leaning over a crossword. But I was demented, going in and out for fags.

The last paper was botany and it had been alright. I wandered around the quad afterwards. A radiant figure in a black raincoat jumped in front of me and I forgot to brush him off light-heartedly.

Carl said that everyone was going to some pub in

Oliver Plunkett Street. Murphy was working behind the bar and giving out free drink. We walked through the streets in the early summer light, with the smell of beer, smoke and burgers. Office-type girls wearing pastel trousers queued up outside the Capitol cinema.

The pub was small, full of hippies. The smell of grass. Heat. Everyone flaming. Murphy wore a huge pair of army trousers held up with red braces, no T-shirt. The sweat glistened on his bare chest, he only needed a pitchfork and hooves.

You had to hand in money when you were getting free drink. Murphy was supposed to hand it back again making it look like change, so I didn't notice at first when Murphy put a big lump of change into my hand. Then I felt the paper crackling in my hand.

'There's a mistake,' I tried to shout over the noise to Murphy.

But the more I shouted at Murphy the more he jumped and whirled. He picked up a broomstick like it was a guitar. *I'm a real wild child!*

The manager was standing just two feet away and I was afraid that Murphy would lose his job.

Rushing down to the jukebox, I told Carl that Murphy had given me the change of a tenner.

'I can't keep the money,' I said.

'Give it to me.' Carl stuffed it into his dungarees. 'Murphy's leaving tonight.'

'But where's his real job?' I asked, remembering the tool-box.

'Murphy's got no real job.' Carl looked at me, surprised. 'He's coming with Jimmy Barry to London. Jimmy only came home for his father's funeral. Murphy's going because there's loads of work in London for the summer.'

'Will he come back?'

'Depends. If the work dries up he'll have to come back.'

About ten minutes before closing time, Claire came in with Best and Jimmy Barry. Saying 'I guess' a lot because she was excited. I worried about her hanging around with Best and Jimmy Barry. Didn't she know what they were doing? She kept giggling. I couldn't figure out if she was unbelievably soft or unbelievably hard.

Claire ordered Britvic. Murphy took her money and I was pleased. I was pleased that she was drinking Britvic because I'd worry about her if she got drunk. And I was pleased that Murphy hadn't given her free drink or the change of a tenner.

After closing time we walked out to Wilton. Jimmy Barry knew someone who was having a party. We couldn't find it though. Carl whispered that Jimmy Barry must have been given a false address. We tried to crash a few nurses' parties, but the minute they saw Jimmy Barry they slammed the door in our faces.

We sat down on the road. Jimmy Barry and Best opened bottles with their teeth. Anyone with an eye in his head could see that Best was mad about Claire. I knew that there was something wrong, but I didn't know if it was my situation or Best's. I was holding Carl's hand.

'Look at the stars,' Carl was saying when he should have been kissing me.

A small van with 'Fitzgerald's Bread' written along the side pulled up. 'Get off the fucking road, ye langers!' roared Murphy at the wheel.

When we got in, a figure was sitting with bowed head in the corner. Fred lifted his ghostly face and I nearly screamed. He knew about a party in Highfield and Carl said it better not be a seance. Murphy drove back into College Road and we were careful this time. We sent Claire to ring the doorbell. She was let in straight away. The house was owned by a crowd of engineers. Savage was the name of the fellow on the door but he had a very mild appearance. He tried to shut us out. Looked amazed when Claire said that we were with her.

Getting in was the last good thing that happened to us. The music was cruel. Jim Croce and the Eagles. Fred and Claire danced to the Eagles. Best slagging them like mad. Delighted to have an excuse to tease Claire, not noticing the romance that was developing over a matter of two or three songs. By the time 'Tequilla Sunrise' came on, Claire and Fred's groping hands were a major embarrassment to me.

The engineers who were having the party were quiet country types. Their hair was neither short nor long and they didn't like having their music slagged off. When Savage told us to get out it seemed to be completely without warning, but Carl said he'd been expecting it the whole time. Didn't I know that Jimmy Barry was only looking for a scrap?

Claire and Fred stopped dancing when Jimmy Barry began to kick the stereo. Best picked up a record and smashed it to the floor. You could see that the violence was really coming from his heart this time. As if that had been a signal, Murphy suddenly punched the quietest-looking engineer and they got into a clenched tussle.

I felt I was growing bristles all over. Fred, Claire, Carl and I slowly began to back towards the hall. Our bodies huge and awkward, each step taking for ever.

The kitchen was hopping up and down, all the engineers fighting as if they'd never done anything else.

The quietest engineer bit Murphy on the cheek.

'You're fucking absurd,' Murphy said and butted him in the chest. I couldn't breathe, I stood watching until Carl pulled my arm and we got to the door and ran out. Jimmy Barry, Murphy and Best came flying out after us, but they couldn't show that they were licked so they picked up stones and smashed the windows. We were cowering in the back of the van when we heard the front door opening and the sound of running feet.

'Get behind the wheel,' Jimmy Barry was shouting at Murphy. I could hear Murphy's boots thudding as he tried to get to the car.

Best was shouting, 'You should have kept the engine running.'

The back doors of the van opened and I didn't recognize the mad faces that started to pelt us with rocks and stones. Carl and Fred tried to cover us, Claire was half laughing, half screaming. I didn't cry out when the stone hit my head, but I nearly died when I felt the warm blood dripping down the back of my neck. My wailing seemed to come from a distance and I wondered if I was having one of those out-of-body experiences that Fred was always talking about. Carl was going mental.

Somehow Murphy managed to get the car started and we got away.

'Your head doesn't half attract bricks, girl,' Murphy said admiringly.

'You're alright, 'tis only a bit of blood, for fuck's sake,' Jimmy Barry snorted, the nearest he could get to consolation.

But they left Carl and me without ceremony outside

the hospital. Opened the back doors for barely a moment, then screeched off. Carl saw Murphy break three sets of lights before they disappeared.

It wasn't much in the end, superficial according to the doctors. I had to wait ages for the X-ray outside a lonely room, miles away from casualty. Claire and Fred came with us. They were kissing a bit. Carl held my hand the whole time.

There was a picture of a stork with a baby stuck to the door of the X-ray room. A notice underneath it said that you were to tell the radiographer if you were pregnant. I went red thinking of Ger and then hoped the others didn't suspect that *I* was pregnant.

The woman who took the X-ray was like someone from the twilight zone. Her hair was bleached hay and she had blue smudges under her eyes. She never spoke, just shot me up and down on a sliding table and lowered plates over my face and the side of my head. The X-ray tube was a weird thing that angled over me like an angry drake.

When the X-rays were ready, the woman finally spoke. 'Take these films back to casualty.' Her words resounded in the empty waiting room like a biblical announcement or a science-fiction threat. I grabbed the films and when Carl asked me why I hadn't said thanks, I said that I wasn't going to thank anyone for giving me cancer and that he'd want to change his violent friends.

'I'd have fucking fought tonight only I was protecting you!' We weren't speaking by the time the taxi dropped me home.

PART TWO

· The Princess and the Pea ·

· *Seventeen* ·

The clinic was an old redbrick house in Brixton. Dusty trees lined the road. I imagined gagged women screaming in agony. Blood flowing down walls.

The first night, we stayed in north London. Ger had to get up at eight to get the tube. I said I was coming too, even though Ger told me there was no need every five minutes.

I had a map of the underground. I liked working out the connections of the coloured grids and diagonal lines. Someone said that it wasn't a realistic map, that everything was out of proportion. But this was the way I liked to think of London. Solid and connected. Northern line, black; Victoria line, sky blue; Piccadilly line, indigo.

Ger said that Pierce thought that the tube was very phallic. I couldn't imagine Pierce in London and I could see that Ger was sorry she'd mentioned it. But when the tube rushed in on a loud breeze, I thought that I understood what he meant. Wild and fierce, John Lydon's eyes. Carl dancing.

We got on the Northern Line first and changed at King's Cross to get the Victoria Line to Brixton. Brixton sounded such a hard place. It had a prison.

Ger was smoking. A tuft of white nightdress peeped out of her small coloured rucksack. She was holding a second-hand Penguin paperback, *Death in Venice*. It had the old-fashioned orange and white cover, with no picture. The price was on the front, 6/-. I was sure that it was one of Pierce's old books from the sixties.

'You're only dying for a chance to mention him.' Ger fixed her skirt violently.

'I'm not!'

'God, you're unbelievable! Imagine going off buying *Wide Sargasso Sea* and reading it under my nose all during exam time.'

'Well, I'm sorry, it's just that I thought that I'd better find out what it was about.'

'It would have been more in your line to do your study.'

If we weren't on our way to Ger's abortion, I'd have said something. The mention of exams made the old dull panic come back. The results were out in a few weeks and Fred said he'd bring them when he came over with Claire. He was talking about seances again. He said that he had some very interesting London addresses. I didn't know how he expected to have a seance with Claire giggling all the time.

The tube lurched in and out of stations. People got in and out. Ger managed to look like everyone else. Cold and bored-looking. I sat bolt upright, staring into the dark windows as if they were revelations.

The tube rocked and oscillated through the different stations: Oxford Circus, Green Park, Victoria. A crowd of punks got on at Pimlico. One of them grinned at me, but I didn't feel too good. They had brilliant coloured hair standing up a mile, loads of studs on their black trousers. One girl had a bicycle chain around her neck and a safety pin through her cheek. They were *real* punks, they made me feel faded. One of them was wearing bondage trousers and they reminded me of Murphy. I didn't know why I still liked him. He was so violent.

At Brixton station, I held Ger's hand. I expected her to push me away, but Ger hung on hard. She was pale. My heart was thudding.

'Let's just get a taxi, and then we won't have to be searching and worrying about the time,' I said, realizing that I couldn't look up my *A–Z* with one hand.

Ger muttered. She looked distracted. As if she was revising for exams again. As if she might start quoting or having visions.

The cab driver had dreadlocks tied back loosely in a piece of bright pink wool. His face was long and thin. Respectful. Like an undertaker, I thought. I watched his long well-shaped fingers on the steering wheel, the purplish nails shining. The radio was really loud. Reggae. He took a pair of sunglasses off the dashboard and hooked them over his eyes. I wanted Ger to say *no* and tell him to turn back, but Ger lit another cigarette.

Ger wasn't sure of the road. We took a wrong turning and had to turn around. I leaned forward to try to help but he waved me back. 'Relax, man, I know this town.'

He looked in the mirror and his black glasses flashed. 'Hey, look out! Your friend.'

Ger was rolled into a ball, clutching her stomach.

'Let me out,' she croaked. 'I'm going to be sick.'

The taxi driver made a sucking noise through his teeth and slowed down. Ger threw herself out the door, nearly falling on the pavement.

I struggled with my door, but the driver was on the pavement in a flash, his hand on Ger's back. I watched the big gold-coin ring on his finger as he patted Ger's black jacket.

'Get yore head between your knees.' His voice went up and down, and the music drifted in the background from his car, still running.

'I'm a trained nurse,' he said to me, as if I was looking for his credentials.

'Nuttin?' he asked Ger in a disappointed voice.

Ger took his handkerchief and wiped her face. He helped Ger gently back into the car. I stared into his dreadlocks. Surely he would say something wise. Something that would change our whole lives. Or stop Ger from going to the clinic.

I began to feel sick myself. The car seemed to be swaying. UB40 came on the radio. 'Red Red Wine'. I felt I was going to puke. I kept thinking something was going to happen before we got there, but we were at the clinic and the driver was helping Ger out.

He gave me his card.

'Nursin' or cars,' he said and pushed his glasses up onto his hair.

When he was gone, I missed the music. The quiet was worse. Around the corner of the house, a middle-aged blonde woman was coming against us, leaning on a man in a grey suit. Her face was just one big wail of grief, the man's wrinkles sunk deep into his cheeks. The woman leaned harder against the man and moaned as if she had lost everything.

I shot a quick glance at Ger but she was stamping out a cigarette.

'The sign says to go to that prefab to check in.' Ger heaved the bag.

'Are you sure?' I suddenly burst out.

'You're a great support anyway.' Ger's pink lips seemed a bit blue.

'Look, I'm sorry, I just can't help thinking, did you see that woman?'

'I didn't see any woman.' Ger threw her bag down on the ground and folded her arms. 'Why don't you just fuck off!'

'You know that I can't!'

'Well, you're going to have to!'

'You might change your mind, I'll support you, anyway.'

'Look, girl, I'll tell you what's happening again, because you don't seem to have got the message! I'm having an abortion, that's what's happening. I'm not having that baby. Pierce is too busy looking after Myra's bad nerves.'

'Please let me stay with you, Ger.'

'You'll be asking to come into the operation next! For Christ's sake let me get on with it!'

Another taxi pulled up and four girls got out, talking in Spanish. They had clear olive skins, they wore soft woollen clothes and carried expensive-looking leather bags. The tallest one paid the cab driver while the others waited for her. They didn't seem upset.

I was staring so hard at the Spanish girls, I didn't notice Ger's tears. When I turned back, she was scrabbling in her rucksack for a tissue.

One of the Spanish girls stopped. She wore a pale pink polo-neck jumper. The softest-looking wool that I had ever seen. 'Tranquilo, tranquilo,' she said, gently.

'She's alright. I . . . am . . . with . . . her . . . amigo . . . of . . . mine.' I nodded at them, speaking slowly, as if that could make them understand. Ger began to laugh through her tears and I gave a nervous giggle at the Spanish girls who were looking at me worriedly. Ger and I moved off towards the prefab.

'I'm going in now. You might as well go,' Ger said, drying her face on my jumper. I didn't know whether to shake her hand or what. I tried to give her a hug, throwing myself awkwardly against her chest. She picked up her rucksack and smiled. 'Go home!' she said, as if I were a terrier. Turning her blotchy face away, she began walking towards the prefab.

By the time I got back to Brixton High Street, I couldn't believe that those Spanish girls, the man with the deep wrinkles, or the shabby prefab had been real. I kept seeing Ger's blotches and the way even her eyebrows had gone red. On the tube back to north London I didn't even look at my new *A–Z* once. The most fantastic punks in the most fantastic gear could have got on the tube, I wouldn't have seen them.

· *Eighteen* ·

It seemed okay when I arrived with Ger, just a shabby one-bedroom garden flat. The students who normally rented it had gone to Europe for the summer.

The front room looked out through railings on to the street and when evening began to fall, I noticed that the front window had no curtains. We hadn't noticed the previous night; we'd gone to bed straight away, exhausted from the boat.

I tried to read, but the main light bulb glared at me and it made passers-by look into the lit room. A middle-aged woman with a huge blonde bun lurched past, then lurched back again for a look. She stopped to light a cigarette, her face haggard in the shadows.

I stood up with my hand over my jumping heart. The woman stared and then picked up three plastic bags and walked off. I looked down the street at the woman's back. She wore a short quilted purple coat. Her long thin neck with its load of blonde, untidy hair looked weird sticking out of the pumped-up coat.

I waited for a few minutes and then, when the woman seemed to have safely dissolved into the distance, I rushed over to the light switch and turned it off. I sat down in the dark and folded my arms.

I knew that I'd seen a lamp in the flat but I couldn't

remember where. I got up and crept into the kitchen. I turned on the light. A poster of the Cure hung over the cooker, curling at the edges. Greasy. It curled even more as I looked at it, waving its feathery edges.

Dry-mouthed, I left the kitchen and went to the bedroom. There was the lamp on top of the wardrobe but I couldn't reach it. I strained on tiptoe and fell against the mirror, frightening myself even more with my close-up face. My spiky-haired rabbit-eyed reflection.

I grabbed a chair and put it against the wardrobe. The lamp was covered in dust. Balls of fluff floated down and clung to my black T-shirt. One ball of fluff stuck to my eyelashes, casting a shadow, making me think for a moment that there was someone in the room with me. I grabbed a towel and rubbed myself down quickly, my hands trembling. Afraid that I was going to start seeing *things*.

The lamp was light, wooden, an imitation candle painted cream. The lampshade was orange. I took it down to the sitting room, stood it on the side table and plugged it in.

An orange glow filled the room, and I was able to read my book huddled in a chair close to the table. I was rushing to finish *Wide Sargasso Sea* before Ger came out of the clinic.

'Justice,' she said. 'I've heard that word. It's a cold word. I tried it out,' she said, still speaking in a low voice.

'I wrote it down. I wrote it down and always it looked like a damn cold lie to me. There is no justice.'

She drank some more rum and went on, 'My mother whom you all talk about, what justice did she have? My mother sitting in the rocking-chair speaking about dead horses and dead grooms and a black devil kissing her sad mouth. Like you kissed mine,' she said.

I couldn't help thinking that Pierce was like a black devil kissing Ger's mouth. Pierce's lips had twice the normal amount of sensitive nerve-endings because his mouth was so long. He must have enjoyed it more than Ger whose mouth was half the length. It worried me a bit the way I was thinking about Pierce. I looked out of the window.

A tall thin Indian passed by and he smoothed his hair as he looked in the window. I thought that his eyes pierced the room and my pulse raced again. *A black devil kissing her sad mouth.* I threw the book to the ground and lay on the floor, where I was sure that I couldn't be seen. I decided to finish *Wide Sargasso Sea* in daylight before Ger came home.

I looked at my watch. Nine o'clock. She had said to ring at nine although I couldn't see how Ger could have known the right time to ring.

I watched the tree outside the window. The lamp's reflection sat in its dark leaves, like a brilliant coloured mirage. The leaves of the tree shifted a little in the slight breeze, but the lamp stayed steady, unshakeable.

I went to get my coat, which hung behind the bedroom door. I checked the pocket for the front door key before I banged the door shut.

As I walked past the sitting-room window, I looked in. The orange lamp glowed dimly in the corner. I could make out the outline of the table among the shadows. Maybe the blonde woman and the Indian man hadn't seen me. Had only been admiring their own reflections.

I knew that there were two phone boxes on the next street. I hurried along, my right hand in my pocket gripping the pile of silver that I'd saved up for this phone call.

It was not a cold night. A pale moon was in the sky, disintegrating on one side. Children shrieked from a little park. One of them started crying, the cries unbearable. Who was looking after them? I ran across the road, crossing into the street with the phone boxes.

The first phone box didn't have a receiver and the second one didn't work after swallowing all my change. I'd a sudden vision of Murphy's tool-box. Weren't Jimmy Barry and Murphy in London somewhere?

I needed to get more ten-pences and the Seven–Eleven was on the next street. I tried not to think it was ominous the way I had to go further and further away from the flat.

In the shop, bright light dazzled and freezers hummed. Kids hung around the counter chewing gum and saying 'fack off' to each other. I bought Rowntrees Fruit Pastilles and ran out with the change and the sweets crushed in my hot hand. At the door a little boy who seemed not more than ten asked me the time.

'Ten to ten,' I said, struggling with the door.

'Sexy legs,' he said and looked round triumphantly at his friends. I looked down at my black drainpipes in horror. One of the reasons I liked being a punkette was because I thought it made me sexless.

A sleepy voice answered the phone. When I asked for Ger there was an abrupt click on the other end of the phone, tapping noises followed and then the engaged sound. Then tapping noises again before the sleepy voice came back on the phone.

'That person has left the clinic.'

'Already?'

'I am not privileged to discuss patients. Please don't ask me any questions. The woman you are looking for has left the clinic.'

'Geraldine . . . Smith.' I fumbled over Ger's false surname.

'She has left, I said.' The sleepy voice got suddenly loud. 'And I'm terminating this phone call.'

The phone went dead, and I stood for a few seconds listening to the lonely drone that sounded down the line. I stood there holding on to the receiver. The word for abortions in England was *terminations*. I couldn't decide whether it made them sound better or worse.

I got out of the phone box. I ran. Buildings hopped up and down, the moon went streaky, an ice-cream wrapper stuck to my shoe and went sluuush sluuush like it had a life of its own. I didn't take it off until I stopped outside the flat and had the courage to bend down. I fitted the front door key shakily into the lock.

Ger was lying on the sofa, her white shirt yellow in the orange light. I didn't recognize her at first. I almost screamed when her tall figure sat up.

'I didn't know that you were coming out tonight,' I said quickly, trying to compose myself. It wasn't fair to have hysterics with someone who'd just had an abortion. I sat down beside her, shrugging my donkey jacket from my shoulders.

'Oh, there was no point in hanging around, and all those Spanish girls never stopped talking and smoking.' It was hard to make out what Ger's face really looked like. In the lamplight it seemed smooth and mellow. But her voice was very tired, almost hoarse.

'Have you got a sore throat?' I asked.

Ger tried to clear her throat. 'It must be the anaesthetic.'

I wanted to hear about the termination. 'You're alright, now, are you?' I asked quietly. Feeling shy about asking directly.

'Just tired, that's all.'

'And it was okay, was it?'

'Was what okay?'

'I mean was it, is it okay to come out so early?'

'Oh yes, yes, there was no problem about that. There isn't an awful lot to it really.'

'But all that money, didn't you pay to stay the night?'

'Jesus, Maeve, it wasn't a five-star hotel, I wasn't exactly missing something brilliant.'

'I know, I'm sorry, I'm just surprised that they let you out so quickly.'

'Actually,' – Ger lay back down on the sofa and smiled up at me – 'they didn't let me out.'

'What do you mean?'

'I just left.'

'Ger!' My heart started going again. 'Oh, Ger, how could you put yourself in such danger?'

'Don't be so dramatic, I'm not in danger.'

'But coming on the tube all that way on your own, what if you fainted or anything!'

'I didn't get a tube, I got a taxi. Pierce gave me extra money before I left. He said to be sure to get a cab home.' Ger snorted as if she had said something hilarious.

'What about the bleeding? What if you start haemorrhaging?'

'It's hardly anything. Come on, Maeve, I can always go to casualty if something happens.'

'Casualty?' I could hear my voice rising despite all attempts to keep it down.

'But I don't need to, I'm fine.' Ger's voice seemed to get hoarser. 'Please, Maeve, don't keep on at me. I'm so tired.'

'I'll make you tea.' I picked up my coat and stood by the door.

'Please.' Ger's voice sank and croaked and she shut her eyes. Her arms went limp.

I went to the kitchen and boiled the kettle. While I was waiting, I decided to fix the peeling poster. Standing on a kitchen stool, I pressed the poster against the blobs of blu-tac with the handle of a bread-knife. It didn't look half so threatening now that it was flat against the wall. Robert Smith didn't seem such a demon.

When the kettle was boiled, I made the tea and opened the packet of Cadbury's Chocolate Fingers that I'd bought in the Seven–Eleven.

As I left the kitchen there was a rattling sound. Robert Smith's eyes were moving. It was only the poster peeling again, but I ran into the sitting room, spilling the coffee over the chocolate fingers.

Ger was fast asleep on the sofa, making delicate, eerie snores.

· *Nineteen* ·

London was hot and airless. We swayed to work every day on the tube. I didn't like it at rush hour. Stuffy. Everyone shining with perspiration. A terrible feeling of bodies. Not the sharp, cold, alcohol-and-perfume smell that came out at night-time. At night it was a different tube that rushed out of the tunnel. Opening sesame doors to exciting half-empty carriages.

Ger was working in a fashionable café in Hampstead. The man who owned the café told Ger that he liked staff that looked weird. Ger didn't seem to mind. She ate a lot of pastries and truffles from the café. She said that she deserved them. That it was hard work having to act weird all the time. Sometimes she brought me truffles and stuff, but they were too rich for me. I preferred ordinary stuff like Munchies and Rolos.

I had a job in the kitchens of a big hospital. One job was scraping the dishes for the dishwasher. I had to scrape them so fast to keep up with the hundreds that piled up beside me that I lost half the cutlery in the refuse bins. The supervisor went rooting in the bins and if she found cutlery would shout at the top of her voice, 'This is coming out of your salary, Mary!'

There was stacking the dishwasher, and sorting cutlery. The worst was standing by the conveyor belt with a jug of gravy in one hand and a jug of custard in the other as dinners rushed past. I lost count of the number of apple tarts over which I'd poured gravy and the supervisor took me off that section. Made me sort cutlery for two whole weeks.

The West Indians were full of sauce and swagger. They were the best. Their accents and the way they shook their big bodies around. I liked to stand close to them and bask when they were giving cheek to the supervisor.

I loved London but I hated work. Once work was over and I'd met Ger, I was fine.

Carl didn't know our address. We just told him that we were going to north London and left without saying goodbye. I didn't want any more violence. Ger said I was dead right, we were supposed to be enjoying ourselves in London. But then we met Best in Piccadilly in an underground Irish pub called Wards.

It was a converted Victorian public lavatory and was supposed to be full of atmosphere. But there was nowhere to sit down. I had to wait all night until someone got off a barrel which I shared with Ger. We had terrible pains by the end of the night. It was just at the end that we met Best. He'd finished his degree and he was on his way to Germany for a job interview. He looked happy to be getting away from his violent responsibilities. He said that he didn't think he'd be coming back to London.

'Or Cork either,' he added.

He gave us Tom and Carl's number. Said that Carl was combing London for me.

'He's not getting very far if he's only got as far as Clapham,' Ger said. 'We *told* him that we were staying in north London.'

Best muttered something about Australian parties

down at Earl's Court. It worried me. Australian girls had shorts and tans. They might even be blonde.

We arranged to meet Tom and Carl on Friday night. That day was the hottest day, eighty-eight degrees. In the tube, the bored faces looked as if they might melt into their clothes. The sticky air pressed down on us.

Lurching through the pitch-black tunnel between Tufnell Park and Kentish Town, the train suddenly stopped. The carriage jolted a few inches, stopped, jolted a few inches more, and then stopped for a very long time.

'You wouldn't want to suffer from claustrophobia!' I said, thinking that maybe I did suffer from claustrophobia.

Ger didn't answer. She took off her purple cotton shawl. Underneath, her black dress clung to her body and waves of musk mixed with the smell of wine from the businessman who sat beside us, surreptitiously inserting his fingers down the back of his tight shirt. His jacket lay across his lap and his pale-blue shirt stuck in rivulets to his chest.

'I don't like this,' I said, feeling repetitive but needing to speak.

'Well, who do you think does? I hate having to take off my shawl.'

'Why?'

'Because I'm getting fat from all those cakes at XT's.'

'You're not a bit,' I said, automatically.

'If you saw me without my clothes,' Ger began and the man in the suit stared at her.

Ger gave me a look and took a paperback out of her bag.

There were lots of things now that I couldn't talk

about to Ger. Not just terminations and *Wide Sargasso Sea*, but loads of other little things. Like Curtains, or books that Pierce had loaned to Ger. And I didn't know which books Pierce had loaned Ger, so I gave up mentioning books altogether. Even the exams. Ger couldn't bear to talk about the exams. She said that she'd been hopeless and it was all Pierce's fault.

I wondered if I should ring home. I didn't mind my mother. I'd probably have liked her more if she hadn't been so caught up in outwitting my father. Running in the front door with big bags of shopping from Limerick. My job was to distract him by doing something really wasteful. Like giving salmon to the cat. I was the decoy. And I had to put up with his rage while she dashed about upstairs hiding her purchases. Rustling noises. Wardrobe doors and drawers going like mad.

Anyway it was stupid. She never got a chance to wear the clothes. She had to wait until he was away which was almost never. Sometimes he went to the All Ireland. Maybe once in three years. Something like that. It was never worth it. And I was branded as a waster. No wonder he didn't want me to go to college.

The tube began to move again and Ger put her shawl back on even though it hadn't got any cooler.

When the train stopped at Kentish Town, Ger leaped to her feet. 'Quick, come on.' She hated getting stuck behind the shuffling crowd.

I preferred to dawdle because I was so tired, but I always went quickly with Ger when she asked me because sometimes Ger looked so pale and I was afraid that she might have complications because of the termination.

We bought Cornettos on the way home, looking

forward to when we got to sit down. We soaked our feet every evening in two bright plastic basins which we bought the first week we got paid. Ger's was green and mine was red.

Ger tuned in to Radio 3. I filled the basins with water and ice cubes. Later we had hot water to wash the dust away.

'Are you going to dye your hair?' Ger asked me, after we'd sat for a quarter of an hour.

'Maybe it's too much!'

'It'll be great.' Ger stepped out of her basin, leaving puddles and pools on the kitchen linoleum.

I sighed, looking at the floor. Another thing that I couldn't point out to Ger. The way she was leaving terrible messes around the flat. I sighed even deeper and stepped out of the basin carelessly. Slopping even bigger puddles.

An hour later, my face was pale and glittery under glossy navy spikes. Ger was making me up, drawing black and dark-blue swipes and curves around my eyes. Putting dark red lipstick on my mouth. I told her I didn't want it and she told me not to be stupid. She found a dress, an old black clingy one that she said was too small for her.

'You know I can't wear dresses!' I said, but Ger made me wear it.

'Do you want Carl to think that you're boring? You can't be always the same.'

There was a huge cigarette burn at the knee and Ger cut the bottom of the dress off until it was half way up my thighs. We sellotaped up the ends and added glue to make sure that it would stick for the night.

When the tube came out of the tunnel, empty carriages ran past us like ghosts. The breeze in the tunnels was cool and warm, cool and warm. Tantalizing. I thought, here I am in London.

· *Twenty* ·

The pub in St Martin's Lane had tall counters and mirrors. I caught a glimpse of my blue-black reflection when I was ordering the drinks, and I held my breath for a minute.

'Two glasses of cider, please.'

The barman gave me a funny look and Ger nudged.

'Sorry, two half pints of cider.' I kept forgetting that you had to ask for half pints instead of glasses. It annoyed Ger. She hated us looking green.

'Why do you keep asking for glasses?'

'I forget,' I said. 'And so what anyway? Are you trying to pretend that we're not from a different country?'

'Ah, you're completely off the point!' Ger said and ordered a packet of crisps.

'You'll have an English accent next,' I said.

'My father had,' Ger said.

'I never knew that he was English.'

'No, he just had an accent. It was probably really dire. I was too young to know the difference.'

The barman smiled and pushed a tray of peanuts down our end of the counter. I smiled back at him and took one peanut.

'For god's sake, don't start flirting now,' Ger said.

'If you mess things up with Carl tonight, I'll never help you again.'

'Flirt?' I said in a heated voice. 'I *never* flirt. I was just being nice.'

'Oh, is that what you call it?'

'What was I supposed to do? Hit him?'

'Maybe it's just the mascara,' Ger said in a suddenly tired voice.

I sat for a minute, holding my blue-black head carefully in my hands. 'What exactly *is* flirting anyway? Could you define it?'

Ger groaned. 'Why do I put up with you?'

'I'm going to ruin everything. I know it.'

'You've got a dangerous attitude for this evening,' Ger warned.

I saw my face in the mirror. My head was like a gigantic bluebottle. I shivered and picked up my glass of cider. Drinking it down, the alcohol seemed to strain along my veins.

'Do your arms get very heavy when you start drinking?'

'No,' said Ger and lit a cigarette.

'Mine do, it's like my blood vessels are being stretched. Don't you get that feeling?'

'Jesus, I don't think I'd drink if it had that effect on me.'

'It's not that bad, I can tolerate it,' I said and drank more cider. The barman smiled at me again and I looked away.

'You're doing it again.'

'What?'

'Flirting with him. Carl will have a canary.'

'I was *avoiding* him!' I said desperately as Carl and Tom came through the tall glass doors.

Carl's hair was scarlet against his white face. His

wrists stuck out of the short sleeves of his thin black jacket. Everyone else seemed half dead beside him. Tom and Carl's eyes were huge in their faces. They were on something. Carl was shivering.

'Fancy a pondy,' Carl said to me. He said that Best had given them a stash. Best was into Blues. He couldn't be bothered with pondies now.

I didn't know. I never took drugs, but if I didn't take them I'd be on the outside again. I held out my hand and Carl told me not to look. I felt his cool fingers piling tiny pills into the palm of my hand.

Ger shook her head. 'I'm too tired.'

The truth was that Ger wasn't taking drugs since the termination.

I saw my shiny reflection out of the corner of my eye in the mirrors as I walked down the bar, but I didn't look at it straight on. I was afraid.

In the toilet I looked at the tiny tablets for a second before they drifted down my throat. I didn't check the mirror on the way out. I didn't want to know if my mascara had run. Carl would have seen it already and that would kill me. It was better not to know.

Carl had a glass of mineral water, but he barely wetted his lips. 'There's no way that I can swallow, now.' He put his fingers around his throat, made faint choking noises. 'The muscles in your throat constrict, you better drink quick before they affect you.'

I took the glass of cider that Ger had ordered and drank it down quickly.

'You'll get cold too, have you got a jumper?' Carl asked.

'The first hour is awful, you're going to feel shite,' Tom said in a half sympathetic voice.

'You won't be able to move tomorrow,' Ger said and pulled her shawl tight as if she was cold.

'You can make my breakfast.' Tom tried to put his arm around her.

'You must be joking.' Ger slipped out of his reach, but she seemed pleased that he'd tried.

'Aren't we staying with you? It's too far to get back to Brixton after we've seen you home.'

'And who says that you're seeing us home?' I wondered if Ger knew that she was flirting.

They were right about the cold. I shivered in my donkey jacket. Carl was swaying in front of me, talking about Elvis Costello. I kept looking at him, checking that nothing was different. His eyes were still gunmetal grey, his hair was still red. I was glad that he hadn't dyed it.

I had a packet of Thornton's treacle toffees in my pocket, but I didn't have the energy to take them out. I knew that I wouldn't be able to swallow them anyway. My throat had tightened and I could barely get a trickle of cider down.

For about ten minutes, I didn't talk. I was frightened and cold. Cold, cold, my arms, my legs. The bottom of my stomach. I couldn't even summon up the energy to pick up my glass. Razor-sharp butterflies began in my stomach.

'It's not long now.' Carl put his hand around my shoulders to cheer me on. His arm felt warm and comfortable. He didn't take it away. I didn't move.

The butterflies moved faster and faster in my stomach until there was a fuzzy blur of feeling and the veins in my legs seemed to buzz. Carl was looking away. As if his arm was such a big part of him, he couldn't be seen to be giving me anything else.

'She's getting it!' Tom shouted and nudged Ger.

Carl turned around and looked at me. I smiled until

the sides of my cheeks were raw from stretching. Carl said something stupid, I couldn't even remember what he said two seconds later. We were all laughing in a really weird, out of focus way. Except for Ger, but she didn't seem to mind. I wanted to talk. I felt witty but I couldn't think of a thing to say.

'You can't stay here,' Ger said.

Carl turned so that his arm was around me and his face next to mine.

We didn't sit down in the tube even though there were loads of empty seats. We stood and hung on to the rails, looking at each other and laughing. My body was tingling, the warm wind rushed down the train, my mouth was sore from smiling. Carl kept holding my hand and Tom kept slagging him because he couldn't hold Ger's hand.

Dingwalls was on Camden Lock and it was smaller and darker than I'd expected. We had to go down an alley. It was the gear knock. Seedy and atmospheric.

The man on the door was deadly. Debauched. He gave Ger the eye.

'Did you see his raddled cheeks?' Ger exclaimed when we got inside.

There were loads of punks and mods inside. The punks stood in groups like they were posing for a photo. Every kind of coloured hair, a couple of mohicans, long chains. Even someone with a swastika armband. I had a swastika armband in Cork but I never wore it because I felt bad about the Jews. One night I *was* going to wear it and Carl said the moment for swastikas had passed. 'No one is going to be impressed by swastikas now!'

Ten Pole Tudor came on, we all rushed on to the

floor. *Deep in the castle and back from the wars, back with my baby . . . oo ra oo ra ay over the hills with the swords of a thousand men.*

We were hot. We took off all our jumpers and jackets. *Oo ra oo ra ay over the hills with the swords of a thousand men.* Carl's T-shirt was sticking to him. Ger still hung on to her purple shawl, but she wasn't really dancing like we were. She drifted around the dance floor. Tom danced with her, but he was so manic that they looked like a couple who'd got separated from their original partners.

Oh bondage! Up yours! We pogoed for a while. Carl and I swung our arms. Ska dancing to 'Oliver's Army'. Carl's long legs were going everywhere. Ger closed her eyes a lot when she was dancing. It was a bit hippyish and I tried not to feel ashamed of her. I wondered if she was thinking about Pierce.

The thought of Pierce dancing in Dingwalls made me smile. They all asked me what I was laughing at but I couldn't say. I thought about Pierce's look of amazement and his long mouth with twice as many nerve-endings and I laughed more. Carl and Tom laughed even though they hadn't a clue what was on my mind. They leaned over and held their stomachs.

I shouted in Ger's ear, 'Aren't you sick of us?'

'What?'

'Aren't you sick of us?'

But Ger shrugged her shoulders, she couldn't hear me. She took a roll-up out of her pocket and lit up.

Ger took charge of us later and shepherded us into a taxi, Cinderellas who had to get home before the magic stopped. The coming down from pondies was supposed to be awful. You had to be in your bed before it started. And that was how I got into bed with Carl, in the mad rush before we turned into pumpkins.

· *Twenty-one* ·

I woke up to a strange dreamy sort of feeling. Carl was awake too, his knuckles ivory handles holding the top of the sheets. Every part of me was dry, not just my mouth but the skin of my hands and the soles of my feet. Every drop of water that ever existed had evaporated. Left us dessicated like two skeletons in a white desert. Even Carl's freckles were bleached.

It was a while before I could get the energy to say, 'I can't move.'

'Neither can I.' Carl's knuckles twitched slightly as if he was trying to prove his words wrong.

'Where's Ger?' I turned my head with an effort to look at the empty bed.

'I don't know,' Carl said and groaned slightly. A sharp sweetish smell made me self-conscious. Was it Carl's smell?

'It's unbelievable, isn't it?' I said, trying to make conversation to hide my discomfort.

'You forget how bad it is,' Carl sighed, 'until you do it again and remind yourself.'

'I'm starving,' I said.

'Do you think that you could shout out to Ger?'

'There's no way I could shout.'

I nearly died at the thought of Ger seeing us in bed together.

'What's wrong?' Carl asked and a chemical smell wafted from his mouth. I wondered if I had the same smell. I didn't mind it, it was chemical, not carnal.

I lifted my hand and let it drop back on to the sheet dramatically. 'Your hands look like a corpse's,' I said to Carl and wondered if I should touch them. I remembered the time I saw my father in his under-pants. Then I couldn't get my father out of my head.

Carl's hand opened wide and held mine for a moment. Then he put my hand against his mouth. His mouth was soft and dry, the skin a little flaky, my father's face was hovering. At a respectable distance. Carl's other hand came around my left breast which had fallen forward. Footsteps came to the door and Ger called out.

I jumped a mile. Carl's hand nudged my thigh under the sheet. Ger came in and looked at us.

She was laughing. 'I'm bloody glad I didn't take any. To be honest, I was tempted.'

'I'd never have guessed.' I looked at Ger, glad that she was talking about pondies.

'You must be joking, I was only hanging by a thread. Tom gave me a terrible time.'

'Where's Tom?'

'He's on the sofa, very weak. We didn't get in until four.'

When Ger went out I was looking at the nice way her long thin back supported the red silk dragon on the back of her dressing gown.

'Has she put up weight?' Carl asked when she'd left the room.

'Ger? No! She's so thin.' I was surprised, but I was thinking about the way that Ger worried about her

149

weight and kept wearing the purple embroidered shawl no matter how sweltering the weather.

Carl went silent and began playing with my fingers, tracing my fingernails with his own thin fingers.

'My hands are awful.' I tried to hide them under the covers.

'They're not,' Carl said. 'I love them.' He kissed them again.

'I like your lips,' I said. 'They're so flaky.'

'Stop taking the piss!'

'No, I mean it.' I put my lips over his. We lay like that for a while because we didn't have the energy for proper kissing. And I wished that this had happened when we weren't on pondies. But then if I wasn't on pondies, I might have got too shy and ruined everything.

Ger came back with two coffees.

'What about food?' Carl asked, and I wondered if maybe he was right about Ger. She did seem puffy or something. Like her hormones were up the spout. She was probably eating all those pastries to make up for the baby she'd given up.

Someone was hammering on the front door.

'Who do you think it is?' I asked, sure that it was my father after tracking me down.

'You better get it before they're gone,' Carl said.

'Who do you think it is?' I said again.

Tom's voice roared from the sofa, 'Will someone let Fred in, he's going to break the door down.'

'Fred!' He was coming with our results.

We could hear Ger murmuring in the hall, her voice low and monotonous. None of the joyous shrieks that I was secretly hoping for.

Then Ger's footsteps as she came back into the room. Flat shuffles on the lino.

'I'm sorry, Maeve.'

'I knew it,' I said, but it didn't make it any better.

'How did you get on?'

'Second class,' Ger said.

'That's brilliant,' Carl said.

'Yes,' I said, but I knew that it was killing Ger. And she could hardly say oh no only got second class, when I had failed.

I made a right fool of myself. Bawling. Saying, 'It's so unfair, they should have given you a first.'

The timid knocking started on the door again. It was maddening. Fred pretending that he wasn't pushy.

'Tell him to go away,' I said.

Ger went out and came back. 'He's really sorry, he wants to help you for the autumn's.'

'Look,' I said. 'Tell him I'm in bed, he can't come in when I'm like this.'

'Oh don't be stupid, he won't be looking at you!' Ger said. Why not?! I felt like shouting.

'You knew I'd failed too, didn't you?' I looked from Carl to Ger.

'No, we didn't, we were really hoping. You know we were, but we'd be fools if we hadn't guessed at this stage.'

'Nobody hoped like I did.' I sank down on the pillows, tears in ribbons down the sides of my cheeks. 'My father's going to kill me.'

Carl pulled a huge handkerchief from under his pillow and wiped my face.

'I was only trying to be sensible doing science. I'd have preferred history any day of the week. I wouldn't have minded the 1916 rising too much. I didn't know that I'd be tortured with test-tubes.'

151

'It's okay, it's okay.' Carl tried to catch my tears with his handkerchief.

'I didn't know that I wouldn't able to cut plants thin enough for the slides on the microscopes. You've no idea how thin you had to cut those fucking slides! You have to have really nimble fingers.'

Ger and Carl kept trying to make the right sounds.

I was filled with dismay. 'Everybody will think that I'm stupid.'

'Einstein failed First Science,' Ger interrupted.

'But what good is that to me when I'm not Einstein?'

'Thank god,' said Carl, but I wasn't going to laugh.

'I didn't know that brains died out when you were nineteen!'

'It must be all the drink,' Carl said, but I still wouldn't laugh.

Tom was calling from the other room and Ger went to see what he wanted. Carl tried to kiss me, but I kept on explaining why I'd failed. How I didn't have the right hold on my scalpel. I'd never had a chance, the zoology demonstrator had me down as a loser ever since the time I'd hacked the rabbit to pieces. The physics department had me down as a smoker and I never smoked except at exam times.

Was my father a prophet? Knowing that I was going to fail? Or was he the cause of it? Had *he* wanted it?

I had a pain in my head from listening to myself.

· Twenty-two ·

At five o'clock, we struggled out of bed.

I was appalled at my reflection in the bathroom mirror, mascara stains like spider webs all over my face, blue streaks on my cheeks, my eyes worn and dejected. I soaped all the marks away. My skin had a yellowish tint under my new navy-blue hair. It expressed my disappointment.

I stood by the bed for a moment looking at Carl.

'Why didn't you tell me my face was covered with black stuff?' I put my hand up to my face. All I could smell was Imperial Leather. Really cat. 'Letting me go on looking like Dracula's bride.'

'But Dracula's brides are beautiful.'

'I've never even seen a Dracula film, can you imagine that? My father was dead against films, all we ever saw was the news, *Outlook* and *Seven Days*. Or cat Irish music programmes. The worst of all was that fool Jimmy Stewart with his blazer and kilt.'

'Didn't you mention *Circle of Fear*?'

'Oh I only saw it once, when my father was gone to Dublin to the Fine Gael Ard Dheis. My mother was wearing a dress she'd bought for a hundred and fifty in Richard Allens and couldn't ever show him. Red silk with a low neck. She looked a bit of a Dracula's bride herself. We were so scared we slept together in my bed and she wouldn't even take the dress off. I kept asking her to take it off and she kept saying what did it matter and I was afraid to tell her that I was afraid of the dress. There's nothing worse than plunging necklines for pure horror, but my mother kept saying that it didn't matter about it getting ruined because she'd never get a chance to wear it.'

'Which one was it?'

'Which *Circle of Fear*? It was the one where all the artists were getting possessed by the devil. And they all got shrunk one by one and imprisoned in coloured glass jars.'

'Were they possessed by the devil? I never knew that.'

'But didn't you see his face in the mirror, every time one of them looked?'

I thought Carl was being superior and rational and he said that he wasn't in the least, that he was terrified of *Circle of Fear*. He was so bad he felt he had to conquer it and he decided to stay up late one night to watch it on his own.

'What age were you?'

'About fifteen. I turned off all the lights just to make sure I was being tested to the full.'

'What was the story?'

'I can't remember. After the first fifteen minutes I was finished, couldn't even turn the television off, made a bolt for my room. I remember lying in bed chewing Juicy Fruit chewing-gum to try to calm myself. I thought that I'd go down at about half past one when the test card was on and turn it off. Then the old man decided to go downstairs for a drink or something. Came storming into my room demanding that I go down and turn off the television that instant.'

'So did you?'

'I couldn't, I was shitless.'

'Did he understand?'

'Let on that I was frightened? No fucking way. I just kept lying on the bed, chewing as hard as I could. Told him that I wasn't his subject and who did he think he was ordering me around. The whole house was up. My mother in her hairnet begging to be allowed to go down and turn it off, *Richard I'm imploring you!* The old man adamant he was going to make an example of me.'

'And what were you saying?'

'Nothing, just chewing away like Jimmy Dean. In the end my kid sister Becky heard what was going on and ran down to turn it off. They heard her screaming. I was so fucking ashamed, she'd do anything for me you know. A big dripping bloody head, she was so tiny and the television up high so she had to put her face right up against the screen to turn it off. The old man didn't speak to me for a month. Then I didn't speak to him for another six months because he wouldn't let me go to Becky when she was having nightmares.'

'No wonder we're all on drugs,' I said, giving myself a little thrill.

So we decided to take more pondies, twice the amount this time because we were so exhausted. We rushed into our clothes. I could hear Tom talking in a low voice. Ger was laughing. Fred was singing.

I stayed behind to make the bed. My black dress lay in a dusty ball in the corner of the room. It looked a mess, covered in fluff with a mass of Sellotape stuck to the hem. The glue showed up yellow and waxy. I stuffed it in a plastic bag. It would go to the dustbin later, when Ger wasn't looking.

I looked in the mirror gingerly, remembering *Circle of Fear.* I got a fright alright, but it wasn't a supernatural one. My face was pure jaundice under my hair which seemed to have lightened from navy to royal blue. My new T-shirt from the Portobello Road didn't suit me after all. I put on a red shirt, some black eyeliner and went out.

I forgave Fred because he looked so sorry sitting there with a short haircut and smoking. And he had a big bag full of bottles from the off-licence. Claire was coming over to London soon. She was sick of her job in her family's delicatessen.

'I take it she passed?' Carl asked. I was glad he asked. I think that he knew that I had tried a few times but the words kept getting stuck in my throat. Fred nodded discreetly.

'I'm not a bit surprised,' I managed to say, hoping that I sounded as magnanimous as I was trying to be.

Tom took out a new pack of cards from his pocket and slung them from one sallow hand to another.

'I don't think we've got time for cards,' Carl said, looking at me. The others couldn't believe that we'd taken more.

'It'll kill you,' Ger said.

'We thought we'd just go to the Green Man for a few pints to get us going.'

'You'll never get going, I'm warning you,' Ger said. 'Stay here and play cards.'

'You'll frighten the paddies,' Tom said. 'You look like freaks, the two of you. Your faces are away too white, your eyes are crazy black holes in your heads.'

'Don't be so personal,' I said.

'I'm for your good,' Tom went on. 'You'll draw attention to yourselves!'

'It'll be packed on a Saturday night,' Ger said.

'We can manage alright.' Carl drained his glass of orange juice.

'I betcha they'll have music, Brendan Shine and Gloria.'

'They might have set dancing,' Ger said. 'Don't go.'

'They'll have a lonesome man with a toupée playing the keyboards and a woman with a beehive singing country,' Tom warned as Carl went to get his jacket.

As we walked down the road, Carl caught my hand. The night was sticky and there was no air. Rubbish drifted along the street. Our hands tingled. A couple of stripy cats strolled cagily along a garden wall. The smell of summer, of warm evenings and trees over our heads. And the smell of Chinese, Indian and Italian food. Fish and chips. Kebabs. Carl said that he'd never taken pondies two days in a row before.

'I thought you were experts.'

'Jesus, who wants to be an expert on housewife's speed? I'd want to be an expert on something a bit more exciting than slimming tablets.'

'Oh,' I said. Why were people always telling me that I wasn't as daring as I thought I was?

I was disappointed when there was no lonesome man with a toupée. No keyboards, no woman with a beehive singing country. It was crowded and there was nowhere to sit. I lifted my weight from one foot to the other. 'Will we go and lean against the jukebox?'

Carl held our drinks, I led the way, carrying our coats.

It seemed stupid to be carrying coats now. We had expected to get cold like the last time.

My skin crept and crawled and crackled as if it was shrinking and was going to burst. As if all my aching organs would fall out, especially my drug-filled sluggish liver. Which would lie dark red and ugly on the worn carpet.

There were Irish accents everywhere, but it wasn't a bit like Ireland. A gigantic tricolour was draped at the back of the bar over a lurid picture of the Lakes of Killarney. Blues and greens that dazzled so much I wondered if they'd used luminous paint.

We leaned up against the jukebox and a man tried to talk to us. I was too tired. Carl ignored him and drank his pint as quick as he could before his throat closed.

'I don't care what you say to me, I only want to hear that lovely accent!' the man said.

'Nothing's happening,' I said. 'Surely we'd have felt something by now.'

'I've loaned more money to people, no one knows how much,' the man said.

'I can't stick it.' I slumped against the jukebox.

'I've loaned more drink, more fags, more sandwiches!'

'Drink up, it's your only hope. Force it down,' Carl said.

The man stood up suddenly. 'Are you leading that little girl astray!'

'He's only joking,' I said. I thought of Jimmy Barry and how he wouldn't put up with this maudlin talk.

Carl stood behind Jim and gave a thin-lipped sneer. I couldn't help thinking that he looked awful attractive.

'I just want to lie down on the ground.' I hung on to the jukebox for support. 'It's a nightmare.'

A thin middle-aged man came up to Carl and touched his elbow. He looked very conservative, his silvery hair brushed back neatly. A dark suit. I was sure he was going to throw us out.

Carl bent his head to listen to what the man was saying. He shook his head. I strained to hear over the twanging of country music from the jukebox.

Carl was shaking his head, but the man kept insisting. Eventually Carl appeared to give in and the man walked away. Carl caught my hand.

'What is it?'

He pointed over to the corner where the silver-haired man stood. A blonde woman of around the same age was smiling at us.

'They want us to have their seats.'

'What?'

'They want us to take their seats.'

'We can't.'

'He says that his wife can't sit while she's looking at us in this state.'

'What did you tell him?'

'I said that we had the flu.'

'Did he believe you?'

'He said that there was a bad flu going around, but he was surprised that we came out in such a state.'

We squeezed in between the middle-aged couple. They were from Cork. We hardly had to say a word to them. They did all the talking. We said yes and no when we got a chance.

They wanted to talk about Cork. West Cork, there's nothing like West Cork and oh Glengarrif and Garnish Island. Had we ever been to Allihies? I was sick and sicker. Carl's lips were getting thinner. Glandore, Clonakilty and the view from Seskin. The beach at Inchadonney. I wanted to shout except my heart was slowing down, my whole system was grinding. And was that where we went to school now, she supposed we didn't know her cousin when she was there. No I didn't. Surprising. No, it isn't. It was twenty fucking years ago. Oh god, I could hardly lift my drink. Even Carl's hair went pale. I wanted to lie on the floor. Were you ever back at Eyries?

Fuck off the two of you! I wanted to be on my own with Carl, I wanted to ask him if his sister's nightmares stopped. The back road from Beara to Kenmare, the goat's path. Fuck off! I wanted to talk about being a failure. East Cork can be nice too, were we ever in Ballycotton? They'd a caravan in Ballycotton one year but it rained the whole time. Torrential rain. Youghal. Carl's eyes were closing into grey slits, like a giant ginger cat.

We stumbled out at eleven with our head reeling. I told Carl we were never going to accept anything from anybody again.

'There is no such thing as a free seat,' Carl said. 'People are fucking deadly.'

'Serpents,' I said.

· *Twenty-three* ·

Carl kept getting me on my own and saying that the time for sex was at hand. It was awful exciting with his long legs everywhere but I was scared I'd get pregnant and he kept saying rubbish. I couldn't tell him about Ger. About the Terrible Example. About the termination.

On the other hand there was the depression about my exams. Even if I could pass them in the autumn I'd no business doing science. And then what could I do? I desperately wanted to be at college. Carl said if I left college, I could become a real punk then. A dirty violent one.

'Not like those streamlined pretty ones you're always admiring on the King's Road.'

'I wasn't,' I said, embarrassed. Afraid that Carl had noticed the cute black-haired punk who'd given me a look.

'That little fart in the pink leather T-shirt! Of course you know what he wanted.'

'I don't.' I thought all this talk about sex lowered us to the level of parents.

I told him that I'd have sex with him if he gave up doing wrecky.

'I've given it up,' he said. Immediately.

'Yeah, but I'm worried about getting pregnant.'

'London is full of opportunities for violence and women who are not full of Catholic guilt.'

'I'm not full of Catholic guilt! I just don't want to have an abortion. They're very expensive.'

'How much?' Carl asked, quick as a flash.

'Two hundred pounds,' I blurted out and put my hand over my mouth.

'I never thought you had it in you.'

'I didn't have an abortion.'

'Who did?'

'I'm not telling, there's no point in asking.'

'I know, it has to be Ger.'

'No!' I wrung my hands in terror. Ger was in the next room. She might have heard him. 'No, look, swear you won't tell anyone. It was Claire!'

'So that's what she's doing in London. Disgusting!'

'Just look at yourself! It's not disgusting, what else could she do? You can't have a baby in Ireland, you'd be arrested.'

'Oh, come on!'

'You know what I mean, and Claire's doing medicine. She couldn't be stuck with a baby.'

'She could have it adopted.'

'You know that's worse than having an abortion and orphans get trampled on.'

'No, no, I wouldn't mind some innocent like yourself or Ger, but Claire is too smart by far. You know she went to bed and everything with Best.'

'So what.' I tried to keep my face impassive.

'Oh, yes. And then went off with Fred in front of Best's nose. No wonder he broke the records.'

'Carl, you must tell no one. I'm the only one she's told and she was flaming when she told me. I don't know if it was true. I'm sure that she was saying it trying to sound wild.'

Maybe it was the way he kept calling round with those bags from the off-licence, but we agreed to let Fred hold another seance. Ger was like a briar. She wanted to know how we let it happen. Tom said not to worry, he'd take care of her and she nearly went mental. Carl said he felt pity for Fred and we all looked at him.

'Yeah, well I feel sorry for the poor fucker trying to reach his parents all the time.'

'I wouldn't feel too sorry for him, he's got Claire remember,' Tom said.

'Is that an advantage?' Ger asked, looking violent.

While we were waiting for Fred, Jimmy Barry and Murphy came hammering on our front door. Jimmy Barry was wearing his old white duffle coat even though it was the hottest night. Murphy was wearing a raggy T-shirt with chains hanging off it and a bala-clava. I recognized him by his muscles.

'Out of the way, woman,' Jimmy Barry said.

Murphy gave me a friendly punch that nearly severed my arm from my shoulder. The heat was rising off them and the small living room was full with the sound of their breathing. They threw themselves down on the sofa and Murphy peeled off the balaclava.

'How's it going?' Murphy's face was purple.

'What time is de old shamozzel?'

'What shamozzel?' asked Ger. Her shawl was wrapped so tight, I could see it cutting into the pink skin of her shoulders.

'The old seance, like.'

'I didn't know ye were interested in the seance,' Tom said.

'Yerra, we thought for a laugh.' Jimmy Barry was trying to look genial which was very hard for him.

'Come on, what are you up to?' Carl asked.

'Nottin, I swear,' said Jimmy Barry.

'The pigs are after us.' Murphy wiped the sweat off his face with the balaclava.

'I told Murphy not to do the roof of that car,' Jimmy Barry said.

'What roof?' Tom asked.

'There was an old soft-top, you know convertible job, Murphy ripped it right across with his knife.'

Carl muttered something about anarchy ruling and I gave him a look.

'Oh, is the missus giving you stick?' Jimmy Barry looked at me.

'I couldn't help myself.' Murphy tried to be modest about it. 'They were going to come after us anyway. Spades supporters. We'd a huge fight with them after the gig. They must have told the cops.'

Jimmy Barry grinned. 'We came to see the Plugs and we'd a brilliant scrap with the Spades. We pulled the bastards off the stage. We went after them and threw petrol over their van.'

'Where did you get the petrol?' I asked.

'Don't ask any more,' Ger said. She looked sick and she was holding on to her stomach as if it was hurting her.

'Are the cops following you?' Tom looked uneasy.

'Naw, we saw them outside the squat and we doubled back. They haven't a clue where we are.' Jimmy Barry sounded confident now that he'd got his breathing back.

Jimmy Barry and Murphy were keen to get on with the seance. We waited and waited for Fred. It went

164

past nine, ten. Tom went out to get some flagons of cider. At eleven, Tom took out his pack of playing cards.

We played 'hundred and ten'. I was useless at taking chances and I never betted above twenty. Jimmy Barry told me that I was pitiful.

I didn't mind Jimmy Barry too much now. He was better when Best wasn't around. All that swaggering. I thought that they must have hated each other really.

When I was a child my favourite book was *The Princess and the Pea*. There were two pictures in the book that I kept looking at. One was a picture of the queen standing on a ladder supervising the servants who were putting the bed together. I really wanted a bed like that. All those mattresses. All different colours, violet, cream, apple green, black diamonds on bright pink. Stripy ones as well. And then the goosedown pillows, the curtains round the bed.

The other picture showed the princess arriving at the castle door in the middle of the storm and the rain. She looked so bedraggled and piteous. Pools of water at her feet. That's what Claire looked like when she came to the front door at one o'clock in the morning. Even though it wasn't raining, her Charlie's Angels hair was stuck to her head, saturated in sweat and tears.

We were at the height of a game of hundred and ten, everyone was shouting.

We thought that she had been followed or some-thing and she couldn't speak at first. Ger offered her cider or even tea but she just shook her head and gave a shiver.

'A glass of water?' I asked and she nodded.

Carl followed me into the kitchen. 'What's wrong?'

'How do I know?'

'Do you think it's because of the abortion?' I looked at him, surprised at the way my lie wouldn't go away.

'No, no!' I put my hands up to my head. 'Look I'm sure she made that story up trying to sound dangerous or something.'

I thrust the glass of water into Carl's hand. 'Take that in to her.'

I followed him and as we arrived in, Claire was saying to the others in a whisper, 'Fred is dead.'

I got a terrible desire to laugh.

All I could think about was a joke that was going round about a singing telegram. You had to sing the punch line, *Fred and the kids are dead woo!*

But no one else seemed to think about the telegram joke. Jimmy Barry's face was a stone. Carl gave Claire the water. Her hand was trembling when she took the glass. With her other hand she pushed back a piece of her hair that was stuck to her cheek.

'It was an accident.'

'Where?'

'Camden Town, about five o'clock. He was rushed to UCH but it was too late. I went in the ambulance with him. I held his hand.'

UCH. I kept wondering about details. I found it impossible to believe that he was dead. Nobody I knew had ever died. Not even my grandparents, they were dead before I was born.

Murphy poured Claire some cider and she held the glass tightly. 'It was on the pelican crossing. We'd got to the footpath when he realized that he'd dropped his wallet, he went back, the lights were flashing orange. A car had come revving up. He just didn't notice. Or realize. I shouted at him.'

Claire started crying again. It began whimpery and

166

then went into a kind of scream. Ger took her into our bedroom and the rest of us sat in silence for a few minutes. I felt like crying but I didn't think that I had the right. I had been mean to Fred.

'Poor fucker,' said Murphy and poured us some more cider. The bottle finished, it trickled off as he poured his own glass.

'Jesus, you never know,' Jimmy Barry said.

I couldn't speak. I hoped that Fred was with his beloved spirits. That they were real and it wasn't all the unconscious. It was unfair to reduce everything through rational explanations. Making us all so small, when really there was nobody that didn't deserve a pair of wings. I sunk into myself. Carl put his arm around me. Life was so delicate. I was nineteen and I'd done nothing. What if I was suddenly swept away?

I could hear faint whooping sounds coming from the bedroom and I thought that I'd better give Ger a hand. When I went into the bedroom, I had to look a second time. There was Claire, doubled up on the bed howling with laughter, her hair hanging into her eyes, Ger leaning up against the wall, tears of laughter streaming down her cheeks.

'Were you joking?'

'No, no, no.' Claire shook her head and went pealing off again.

Ger said not to tell the others they were laughing. Ger tried a few times, wiping her eyes but she only got as far as, 'It's a secret. Claire doesn't want anyone to know . . .'

I was getting really mad when Claire sat up, shook the hair out of her eyes and forced herself to speak.

'It wasn't his wallet that he went back for, it was his bag of letters.'

'What letters?'

'The letters for the ouija board. Nobody must know. I don't want people making jokes about Fred,' Claire said. 'Oh Fred!' She threw herself down again. Laughing and laughing. And you could see the laughter was giving her a terrible pain in her chest and stomach.

Guilt about the lie I'd told Carl was affecting my own breathing. I had a cramp in my stomach. I went out of the bedroom again, and I could have been invisible for all the notice that Ger and Claire took of me.

Murphy and Jimmy Barry were passing round some blues they'd got from Terry, an English punk who dealt in speed. I beckoned to Carl to follow me into the kitchen.

Carl's face was snow-white. His grey eyes as dark as anything.

'Look,' I said. 'I told you a lie.'

'When?' Carl pushed his long fingers through the red stubble on his head.

'It wasn't Claire who had the abortion, it was me.'

'Jesus, I don't believe you.'

'No, I'm telling you. That's why I can't have sex. You have to take complete rest from sex for six months.' My nose twitched. I scratched it.

'Hell! Who was it so?'

'Who was what?'

Carl swallowed. 'Who was the father?'

I'd forgotten that it needed to have a father and, groping round quickly in my mind, I almost said Fred. Then I collected myself and said, 'Pierce.'

'Pierce,' said Carl in disgust. You mean he was sleeping with both of you!'

'What two?'

'The whole of college knew about him and Ger.'

'Oh,' I said. 'I didn't know about that until very recently.'

'And were you jealous?'

'No, not really,' I said truthfully.

'Well, I'm fucking jealous!'

'There's no need,' I said. 'It meant nothing to me.'

'You bitch, I thought that you were really innocent and I've been so bloody patient. I suppose you were having a great laugh.'

I thought that I could see tears in his eyes. I wanted to cry myself.

Carl paced up and down the kitchen. His lips disappeared into his face. I was afraid that he'd break something. 'If you hang on a minute, I'll tell you the truth.'

'This is supposed to be the truth,' Carl growled, but he'd stopped pacing and looked half hopeful. His eyes. They were shining from the Blues he'd taken. I didn't want to lose him.

'Swear you won't tell anyone,' I said.

'I swear,' said Carl. 'But I'm fucking exhausted from this, you'd better not perjure yourself any more.'

Carl believed that I hadn't had an abortion but no way would he believe that there wasn't something going on between me and Pierce.

'Not that I give a fuck of course, I just don't know what you all see in him.'

'But he's cat,' I said, and that's where I went wrong because Carl remembered that Ger had always said Pierce was cat too.

· *Twenty-four* ·

Jimmy Barry and Murphy rushed back to Cork for Fred's funeral. Of course we all knew that they were on the run from the cops, but they did go to the funeral. They sent us a postcard from Patrick Street, telling us that everything went off okay.

'Wouldn't surprise me if Fred starts trying to contact us now when we get back. He'll probably head straight for your flat,' Tom said.

'Don't say that!' Ger said.

'You know, I'm only joking,' Tom said. 'Fatty,' he added affectionately and tried to pull her shawl off.

Fred's death had left its mark though. We were very quiet for a few weeks. Claire had gone back. I was going to repeat my exams but I didn't think that I had a chance. My father's face loomed: PASSPORT! PASSPORT! YOU HAVEN'T PAID YOUR TOLL.

Carl now suspected that I had unfulfilled fantasies about Pierce. Of course being a psychologist, Carl had never believed for one second that I would be capable of a real physical relationship with anyone.

On the boat, Carl, Ger and I had Pullman seats. Ger had brought the money out from nowhere, and insisted. Other people lay on the floor on sleeping bags and blankets. Skinheads, punks and hippies. The people with cabins hardly gave them a glance as they went by with their big blocky key rings.

Carl was falling asleep. Ger kept watching him. I was uneasy. And every time Carl seemed asleep, he jerked awake and said, 'What! what! what!'

I looked out the porthole. It was the deadest black out there with the odd bit of grey lace from the waves. I could feel myself drifting into a half dream, when Ger shook me and I jumped.

'What is it? What is it?' I said, half cross. Carl began to stir.

Ger caught my hand, 'Shhhh, don't wake Carl.'

'Why? What's up? Are you sick?'

'I want to talk to you.'

'About what?'

'We'll have to go somewhere else. I don't want Carl to hear.' I hated leaving Carl even for a minute. 'Talk away. He's out for the count.'

'Please, Maeve. I can't talk here.'

I stood up reluctantly. I knew that I had to support her in case she went mad from the termination.

'You'd better bring a jacket.'

'No, I'm fine.' I waved my arms in the air. 'It's very hot.'

'It won't be hot on deck.'

'Are we going up on deck?'

'Maeve, it's only for ten minutes. I wouldn't ask you unless I really had to.'

I gathered my jacket under my arm and followed her across the floor that rose on a gentle swell. We staggered for a minute and then righted ourselves, holding on to the iron bannister of the stairway that led to the upper deck.

Ger stared down into the blackness of the sea. The waves didn't look grey out here. The white ruff that the ship cut into the sea was beautiful. I hoped she wasn't thinking of throwing herself in.

'What is it?' I whispered at her elbow.

'I'm pregnant.'

'What? Tom?'

'Don't be silly, I did nothing with Tom.'

'But how?'

'It's Pierce.'

'But, did he come to London?'

'Oh god, Maeve, I thought that you'd have guessed. Can't you see how fat I've got? I'm *still* pregnant since the first time.'

'Jesus, and that clinic was so expensive!'

'Christ almighty, Maeve, I didn't go through with it.'

'Oh.' I looked at the sea, the way it curled and went up and down. Beautiful in a hard way.

'But what are you going to do? How will you manage?'

'I don't know.'

'What made you change your mind?'

'I don't know really. I just kept imagining it. A little girl, chatty, half bossy and spoilt, cute as hell. Ten years old.'

'That's weird.'

'What's weird about it? *You* don't know what it's like!'

'You're fierce brave.'

'It's probably completely stupid. I don't want to give up English either. I want to have the two of them.'

'Pierce and Tom?'

'The *baby* and my degree!'

'Yes, the baby.'

'I couldn't do it in the end. They were going to suck it out with a hoover.'

'Where did you go all that day?'

'I went to Hampstead.'

'Why didn't you come back? What did you do there?'

Ger ignored my first question. 'I went to Keats's house.'

'That must have been nice.' I looked at the sea. They were going to *hoover* the baby out.

'Oh I was over the moon,' Ger said sarcastically and then, after a minute, 'It was kind of nice in a way.'

Ger was silent again and we listened to the ruffling sound of the water against the side of the ship.

'There was so much hair.'

I couldn't speak, I tried to nod in an understanding way. Ger's face loomed white in the dark.

'There were all these locks of hair, mostly belonging to Fanny Brawne.'

'Who was she?'

'Keats's fiancée. They never got married.'

'That was sad.'

'And the hair, they plaited it and did all sorts of things with it. They had these artists in hair. They specialized in making all these designs with locks of hair.'

'God!'

'There was a little brooch there that Fanny had owned. In the shape of a Greek lyre. The strings were made of Keats's hair. You could barely see the hairs. I had to turn my head on one side to see them.'

Ger's voice rose and fell. 'I wanted to stand in the garden on the spot where he wrote "Ode to a Nightingale", but you weren't allowed to stand on the grass.'

'That was a pity.'

'The original plum tree was gone. I was going to

stand on it anyway, I thought fuck them, but then I started crying and I left.'

Ger sighed and went on. 'I went to Hampstead Heath then. Everywhere I went there was a book to think about.'

'What did you think about on Hampstead Heath?'

'*The Woman in White.*'

I kept worrying about Carl. If he woke up and missed us. I wished that I had a watch to check the time. And I felt guilty for thinking about Carl when Ger was in deadly trouble. Even though I was useless at touching people, I stroked Ger's back. For a long time it seemed. Over and over, like the black and white waves that rushed this way and that. All that night, going back to Cork.

PART THREE

· *The Bushel* ·

When between her and her foes
A mist, a light, an image rose,
Small at first, and weak and frail
Like the vapour of a vale.

Shelley, *The Mask of Anarchy*

· *Twenty-five* ·

We had to go back to the same flat because we'd asked the landlord to keep it for us. Ger didn't want to have to face new landladies in her state.

The flat didn't seem to be haunted any more, just awful sad. I thought that the knocking might have been caused by Ger's unborn foetus insisting on being born. And now it didn't need to insist seeing as it got its own way. Carl said that it could have been my unconscious rebelling against science. I said if that was the case, it would be going insane now that I had to face the repeats. Throwing us out of our beds. Ger said that Fred was at peace now, it was Fred's overwhelming desire to be with his dead parents. She showed me one of Keats's last letters, how he couldn't wait for the cold earth and the daisies to be lying over him. I read it a few times after that. I worried that I might be a bit morbid but it didn't stop me taking the book to bed.

Then Ger showed me another letter that Keats wrote about his girlfriend Fanny Brawne when he was dying. For his last journey to Italy, she made him a travelling hat, and he said that the silk lining scalded his head, because he was never going to see her again. He wrote *Oh God, oh God, oh God* in his letter and it wasn't a bit sickening, only broke my heart. I wondered what Ger's mother would think of *that* for a dangerous letter. And the more I looked at his letters, the more I thought that they *were* shocking and couldn't figure out whether he was self-indulgent or the gear knock. The gear knock, I decided, trying to ration myself to one letter a day while I was studying.

Keats couldn't bear to hear about Fanny or read her letters. I'd a suspicion that Ger was in the same boat over Pierce in a different way.

Neither of us could help it, but we began to get a bit romantic about Fred. Not that we thought that he was a literary hero with coals burning in his breast or anything. I was burdened with feelings of guilt. Half the time I was wondering where those physics notes of his were. I could hardly ask Claire for them though. And then the rest of the time I spent wishing that I'd been nicer to him.

We went up to the grave in Glasheen one evening when Ger felt safe under the cover of darkness. I was surprised to see no headstone, just a clean mound of fresh green, with flowers like a bed you'd dream of. I thought of Keats. Ger said the headstone usually took a year. Fred's grave was all fresh flowers, there were none of the awful plastic ones. There were a few bad examples near Fred's grave. You couldn't even see the flowers under the big plastic covers, like pudding bowls covered with condensation.

We put flowers on the grave and a dog howled in the distance. I jumped, felt like shrieking and running off down the road with Ger, but I restrained myself. It would have been in bad taste, like asking Claire for those very useful physics notes. I didn't remark on the brightness of the moon either, in fact we hardly spoke on the road back. We went to bed quickly. Silently. I knew if we gave the flat half a chance it would go back to its old spooky tricks. When I spoke about it in daylight, Ger said she felt exactly the same way.

'I was sure you were going to ruin it, I can't believe that you'd the sense not to speak,' Ger said and I couldn't credit her insolence.

We were moody hanging around the flat and we'd plenty to get moody about apart from Fred. Ger sat around, reading. I wasn't allowed to mention Pierce and we spent most of our time arguing about Ger going to the doctor. Ger said there was plenty of time, but she was nearly six months now. She'd got the book list for next year and was working her way slowly through *Moby Dick*.

I studied for my repeats. Mostly at the flat. Mainly to keep Ger company. Carl came round to help me with maths and I had physics grinds again. I tried not to think of my father. I tried not to think about what I'd do if I failed. I was worried about money. I argued with Carl.

Ger's hair shone and it grew thicker. She stopped feeling sick and she was walking straighter. Her blood glowed through her skin. I couldn't help wishing that Pierce could see her now.

I hadn't been to Curtains. Ger wouldn't allow me, and I hadn't the heart to defy Ger about anything now. In three months Ger was going to give birth to a baby. It frightened me just thinking about it. All that pain, and how was Ger going to keep going to college?

Ger said that it wasn't a problem because she was going to put the baby in one of those knapsacks that leave your hands free. Take it to lectures. But women who had babies were laid up for ages afterwards. What if the baby cried?

Ger hadn't left the flat for a whole week. She said that she didn't want everyone gawking at her stomach, and she couldn't bear it if she bumped into Pierce. I wondered if I should get a book on home deliveries. But I didn't want to do it. Sending Carl to the kitchen to boil up water, tearing up sheets. Cutting the umbilical cord! We'd lost Ger's good pair of scissors. All we had for cutting was a Kitchen Devil knife and blunt nail clippers that hung on the end of Ger's key-ring.

Ger was pouring milk into the coffees. I could see how quickly her stomach was growing. Even Carl was looking at it.

Ger put sugar in her coffee. 'Stop looking at my stomach!' she said suddenly, without even raising her eyes.

Carl and I looked down at our coffees. Carl was scarlet, and he kept looking at me. Mad because I hadn't told him.

'No wonder I don't want to go out, when the two of you can't keep your bloody eyes off it.'

'You could just go to the hospital,' I said. 'It isn't far and you have to go to those postnatal things some time.'

'I keep telling you it's *ante* natal,' Ger said, snappily. '*Ante* means before and *post* means afterwards.'

'Well, it will be post soon enough.' Carl had recovered quickly from his shock.

'Oh, don't you start,' Ger said.

Carl frowned at her and thought for a minute. 'Do you know who I saw this morning?'

'Who?' I asked.

'Guess!'

'I don't know if I want to,' Ger said and went red.

'Was it Pierce?' I asked.

'Well, what's so unusual about seeing Pierce? I've seen *him* about ten times since we came back.'

'Have you?' blurted Ger quickly and then started biting the skin on the side of her finger.

'No, it's someone who you wouldn't expect to see on Patrick Street.'

'Get on with it,' Ger said.

'Myra!'

'But she never goes outside the door!'

'Not any more by the looks of things! I called into Curtains for a pint and it's Josie who's been getting her out and they're spending a fortune on clothes. Pierce is cracking up.'

'Good,' said Ger, and drained her coffee cup quickly. Her hand shook and she spilt some coffee on her chin. I had to give her a handkerchief.

'I hope she's not spending all his money,' I said indignantly.

'Why do you care about his stupid old money?' Ger asked crossly.

'Well, *you* should because . . .' my voice petered away, as Ger stared.

'Pierce's money does not concern me.'

'It should,' Carl said. 'How are you going to manage otherwise?' I gave him a look. He wasn't supposed to know about Pierce.

'I *will* manage.' Ger put her lower lip out like a step-ladder.

'Look, the main thing is that you go to hospital,' I cut in again, afraid that Ger was going to cry.

'Yeah, why can't you go?' Carl asked. 'Don't you think it's a bit ironic now that Myra is getting out while you're locked up in here?' Ger flicked through

181

the pages of *Moby Dick*. You could see that it was killing
her that Myra was out and about. She didn't speak for
ages afterwards. Just stared at *Moby Dick* without
turning a page.

Best came round later. He hadn't got the job in
Germany. We didn't recognize him at first, he was
wearing a suit. His hair had grown a bit.

'Hey get out, for fuck's sake.' Carl thought that it
was some kind of joke when Best said he'd joined his
father's firm of wine merchants.

'I have to work, boy.' Best was hardly ashamed.

Carl kept looking away and looking back again. 'I
know the danger is there for all of us. But, Jesus, did
you have to do it so quick? I mean, god almighty.'

I was afraid that Carl would go off doing wrecky in
disgust. 'That's a nice suit,' I said.

'Maeve!' shouted Carl.

'For a wine merchant,' I finished lamely.

Best was laughing. I saw him give a quick look in
our brown-spotted mirror. I was glad that he wouldn't
get much of a reflection.

He looked at Ger's stomach. 'I heard you were
poled.'

'Fuck off, Best,' Carl said.

Best was like a bad dream. 'Anyone called to Curtains lately?' he asked with a too innocent face. When
he was gone, Ger announced that she was going to
the hospital.

Everyone knew about Ger and Pierce. Everyone except
Tom who had refused to believe it. Tom rushed out
of the house, cursing and swearing the night we told
him that Ger was pregnant. He came round every day
and gave Ger dog's abuse. We told Ger that she

shouldn't take it so lightly but she said that she felt sorry for him. His mother was drinking heavily with Myra. I think she was trying not to upset the baby.

Jimmy Barry punched the wall when he heard about Best. 'That's what ye're all going to do. Go back to yer mammies and daddies with yer degrees.' He nursed his ballooning hand.

'I'm not going back to any mammy and daddy with a degree,' I said.

'Yerra, don't mind you. You're a weirdo.'

Murphy said he didn't care if Best drowned himself in a wine vat. 'He's a bad fucker. I always knew it.' He picked his nose quickly and looked at us with his stone-coloured eyes. 'What I want to know is are ye definitely jagging now?'

Carl said, 'Don't answer him, Maeve.'

Jimmy Barry offered to make a cradle for the baby.

'Really?'

'Sure, I'm a qualified carpenter,' Jimmy told me and then laughed at my rapturous face. 'Y'oul eedjit. You'd believe anything. Do you think that I'm gone soft in the fucking head?'

He looked at Ger then. 'I'm not that good. I'll put up a few shelves if you like though.'

Ger said thanks but we didn't know if we were staying or not. The landlord didn't know about the baby yet.

· Twenty-six ·

Ger went to the hospital the day before my exams started. Carl said he'd come round to do maths with me.

Ger went off on her own. She wouldn't let me go with her and I needed to be studying anyway. All afternoon I waited and Carl never came. I began to copy the drawing of the camel from my packet of Noah's Ark pencils. I must have drawn twenty and I began to get quite good at it. But then I got frantic and the camels' bumps got wobbly, their faces got anguished and human-looking. I waited. I drew. I paced. I looked out the window. The Angelus bell was ringing when Ger arrived home.

'I didn't know that they'd take so much blood, but I acted as casual as I could. The syringe was cat the way it rested against my arm. The blood was dark and so hot it made my stomach strange. It felt like there was something inside it, climbing like an escalator. The nurse was nice and everything, but then she said something about me being a lot better than the cowards who go off to England to have abortions and I got so upset, and she kept rubbing my back, saying, "Don't mind them, don't mind the feckers." I had to stare really hard at the material of my dress to stop the tears.'

'Oh there's narrow-minded people everywhere,' I said, trying to sound philosophic. But I didn't feel philosophic. Not one bit.

'When I was waiting then for the doctor there was a little boy on his mother's lap, rubbing his mother's face and it was the first time I thought, you know, this might be alright.'

Ger looked down at my camels then. 'Jesus did you do those! They really do look like camels.'

'Do you think so?' I was thrilled for a minute and then Ger caught sight of the worried-looking camels and laughed. 'Those ones are a bit avant-garde, aren't they?'

'Go on, what did the doctor say?' I was disappointed about the camels.

'Oh you know, should have come sooner. She was fine really and she had a thing where I could hear the heartbeat really loud in the room. It was as if she said hocus pocus, I couldn't believe it. I waited hours for the scan, I had to drink loads of water and they showed me the little face sipping the amniotic fluid in the uterus. Dainty! Just like a kitten. It kept moving its arms and legs, turning away from the probe, as if it was annoyed. Like a real person. I have the picture here.'

I thought that the picture was beautiful. The little hand was waving. I told Ger that the baby had beautiful features and then burst into tears. Ger was really moved and it was very embarrassing explaining that I was crying because Carl hadn't turned up and I'd rung his home and his mother answered and I felt deadly. Ger said that he was probably gone somewhere with Tom and I said that he couldn't when my exams were tomorrow. I had maths first and that was why Carl was coming over and he was supposed to be there at two. She kept saying that he was probably with Tom and it drove me mad. He'd probably been arrested for wrecking cars and Ger said if he was with Tom there was no fear of that because Tom was a desperate coward.

Ger propped the ultrasound picture against a vase on the mantelpiece. I stood in front of it studying the shape. The more I looked, the more it became blurred. I kept looking out the window hoping to see Carl coming up through the wild garden like a fugitive, even though he never came that way and the back door was stuck.

Ger must have been desperate to cheer me up because she decided that if we put all our weight against the door we might force it to open and then we could sit out in the garden. We undid the bolt for the first time since we'd moved into the flat. I was afraid for Ger, but after about five minutes of pushing between rests, the wooden door lurched open and we walked out into knee-length grass. A sparrow flew across the garden and we could hear the birds singing.

I liked the September air. 'Bittersweet,' I said.

'Oh yes,' Ger said, but I knew that she was thinking about the little blurry white hand on the negative.

The sky was light blue and a tiny slice of moon had appeared in the east. We brought out chairs and had our supper in the garden. It was more of a wasteland really, the grass nearly up to our waists when we sat down to eat.

We talked about the landlord and what he would do when he found out that Ger was pregnant. We spoke about Fred. We imagined that he was sighing in the wind, and then we had to go in because we'd frightened ourselves.

Ger wrote to her mother. She said it wasn't as hard as she thought it would be. For once she was glad that they didn't have a phone. Give her mother a chance to compose herself. I imagined Ger's mother with her red hair crying over her sewing machine, but Ger said that her mother *never* cried, she would just be terrified someone might read Ger's letter. The envelope was thick and shiny with Sellotape when Ger had finished sealing it.

I went to bed early but I couldn't sleep so I went downstairs to talk to Ger. But Ger didn't want to talk, she was reading Emily Dickinson. Then she insisted on reading one of the poems aloud, even though she must have seen that she was really embarrassing me.

A great Hope fell
You heard no noise
The Ruin was within
Oh cunning wreck that told no tale
And let no Witness in

The mind was built for mighty Freight
For dread occasion planned
How often foundering at Sea
Ostensibly, on Land

And not admitting of the wound
Until it grew so wide
That all my Life had entered it
And there were troughs beside

The closing of the simple lid
That opened to the sun

Until the tender Carpenter
Perpetual nail it down –

She was still mad about Pierce. 'I just wanted to show him the picture of the baby!' She was trying not to cry. That was when I decided that I was going to tell Pierce.

I drank a load of Benylin to make sure that I got a good night's sleep. Ger said that I was hellbent on a path of destruction. 'Look who's criticising,' I said, as I finished the bottle.

· Twenty-seven ·

I woke heavy, my head like a wooden block. Staggering to the bathroom, I threw open the window and looked out on the garden. I remembered the way the wind had sounded like Fred's voice. I wondered what he looked like after the accident. Murphy and Jimmy Barry had seen the body at O'Connor's Funeral Home, but it wasn't the kind of thing you could ask about.

I looked down at my body. Useless. My head clogged with Benylin. I'd been nowhere, done nothing. Except for London. I hadn't been much of a punk there either. I wasn't a dirty, violent punk. I wasn't a high-fashion King's Road one. I was a middle-class watery punk who couldn't even spit properly. And anyway, punk was finished by the time it started.

Trying to be a real punk was like trying to find a real princess. Like feeling a pea under a heap of mattresses. Like trying to ride a horse up a glass mountain. That's why punk drew us all. Why we were all still obsessed with it three years after the Pistols broke up. Why all Ger's favourite poems were by unrequited lovers. Impossible things were the gear knock.

I wanted to pass my exams so that I could stay at college learning things. I wanted to learn so much.

But a horrible black part of myself stopped me. If my father had shut up about money for one minute.

But look at Fred. He'd spent all his time at college, he said that he was a perpetual student. The irony of it, and still no sign of Carl coming up like a fugitive through the garden.

I longed for the end so that I could start again, but I was scared too. I rested my elbows on the window-ledge and shook my head hard. Nothing worked. I had a head of sodden wool. I pulled my head back in.

As I went down the stairs, Ger came out of her bedroom. Her hair tangled. Fumbling with the belt of her red dressing gown, she followed me downstairs.

Down in the kitchen, the air was cold and hard. I had the sensation of almost waking up. Impatiently, I shook a mound of coffee into my mug.

'I'll walk with you to the Aula Max.'

'Don't Ger, go back to bed, I'd prefer to go on my own.' I picked at the spikes of my hair, restlessly.

We sat for a while in silence. The sun got stronger and shone through the kitchen window, showing up the grease on the stove. I got my log tables and my pencil case.

'No point, I suppose, in bringing a book now?' Ger asked.

I shook my head and walked into the bedroom to get my donkey jacket. When I got into the bedroom, I shook my head violently to try and clear it. Pain shot through. I had to grab my head quickly, hold it steady before it flew off.

Out into the sunny September morning, the air smelt beautiful, like ironing. I looked at my log tables, I'd got to like them when I was doing my maths with Carl. Now I hated them even more than I had in the first place.

'Maeve, Maeve.' At first the shouts were so far away, I ignored them. When they became louder I looked back.

It was Carl wearing his black raincoat, shouting and waving. His long skinny legs loping along. I stopped to wait for him. But as he came nearer, I saw his face, the way his eyes looked huge after pondies or drinking. I was sure that he'd been doing wrecky. We had a dog on the farm which looked like that when he came back from chasing sheep. Trigger was a golden cocker right off the front of a box of chocolates. I started running. Trigger wouldn't stop no matter how much we pleaded.

'Maeve, Maeve!'

My father beat Trigger until he bled. *You're breaking my heart*, my father told Trigger.

I pounded along the pavement and crossed the road. A car braked and sounded its horn. I didn't care, I kept running. Trigger had to be put down in the end.

When I got to the other side, I looked back. Carl was halfway across and stuck. A stream of traffic blocked his path. With a small cry of satisfaction, I ran through the college gates and up the steep avenue.

Trigger's face pressed against the back window of our Morris Oxford the day my father drove him to the vet's. My father, coming back bawling, Trigger's corpse in a cardboard box with 'Chivers Marmalade' written in blue letters along the side.

In the quad, crowds of students were walking around with books. I dashed up the steps of the Aula Max.

'Maeve, Maeve!' Carl swept across the quad, his black raincoat flying around him. The students looked up from their books.

I banged through the wooden doors.

Think about the poor frightened sheep, my mother said to us when we were crying after Trigger.

There were still fifteen minutes to go. I laid out my log tables and my pencil case on the rickety table. Folding my arms, I put my head on my hands and waited for the exam to start.

I could smell Trigger, I could hear him whining. I could feel my nose cold against my wrist. I shut my eyes tightly, and tried to shut out the image of Carl's face. Gold and grey and white and red. Like Henry the Eighth when he was young and thin.

I felt a hand on my shoulder.

'I shouldn't be doing this, but your brother is outside. He says that he's got an urgent message for you.'

I looked at the man's name badge: *Mr Coffey, Invigilator.*

'But I haven't got a . . .' I started. I sighed and followed Mr Coffey to the main exit.

'Two minutes,' said Mr Coffey and went back to his desk at the top of the hall.

'Maeve, I know you're mad, but I just want to wish you good luck.'

Stale alcohol fumes wafted as he spoke.

'You've been drinking,' I whispered, fiercely, and then had to stand back to let two long-haired girls through. The girls stared at Carl as they passed.

Carl's lips were flaking and he kept licking them. His mouth was red as if he had been eating raspberry lollipops.

'Maeve, I know that I've let you down, but I want you to get this exam.'

'You only want sex,' I said, mad as anything from the fumes of whiskey.

A tall black-haired fellow with glasses passed between

us, staring at me. 'Big ears,' I said and he backed into the room with his hands in the air. I could see *Mr Coffey, Invigilator* craning to see what was going on.

'Good luck,' called Carl as I turned away.

I went back to my table, shaking. Useless.

'Right, all books on the floor.' Mr Coffey looked tired. 'I'm giving out the exam papers now.'

The adrenaline came to me then, but my brain was jumbled. I had done every problem that came up on the exam paper and it was the worst thing that could have happened to me. I didn't know which one to choose.

I started with question one and worked through it jerkily, my mind whirling. I kept thinking about failing and passing, I kept hoping that I was doing it right. I found it hard to concentrate.

After question one and two, I felt breathless and my hand shook. I looked at the clock. It was quarter past eleven. I had only one more question left to do and the exam finished at half past twelve. I put up my hand.

Mr Coffey came down.

'I need to go out for five minutes.'

'Do you have to?'

'I need fresh air.'

'Okay.' Mr Coffey made a sign to one of the other invigilators and led the way to the door.

Carl was sitting on the ground outside the hall. He looked up anxiously as I passed. I could see by his face that he didn't approve of me coming out. Well, damn you, I couldn't say.

Mr Coffey didn't approve either but he lit a cigarette and said, 'There's no air in that room.'

I didn't stay long, just gulped down huge drags of

tobacco, conscious of Carl's rangy figure watching every puff. He gave me a weird, twisted look when I went back in. He wanted to make up, but he was raging with me for coming out. Up yours, I couldn't say as I went back in again with Mr Coffey.

'That's a devoted brother,' Mr Coffey remarked as he turned the handle of the door.

The only thing that consoled me after the exam was how bad Carl felt. He bought me a box of Maltesers and tried to give it to me discreetly when I came out of the Aula Max. I shrugged the red rattling box away and punched him on the arm. 'You'll never get sex from me.' The tall black-haired fellow with the glasses passed us again, still staring at me. I gave him a look and turned back to Carl. 'Oh don't bother to try and keep in the laughing, I can see you.'

Carl kept trying to grab my hand. His hands were smooth and cold.

'You went out drinking and I didn't know where you were. I was holding my breath all night. I'm not going to do that again.'

'I won't do it again.'

'But you said that you couldn't help it. So how can you stop that happening again?'

'Look, Tom gave me whiskey at twelve o'clock, I was stupid to drink it.'

'You *are* stupid, it's just as well I'm going to fail my exam anyway.'

'Maeve!'

'And I've made up my mind. I'm going to become a nurse.'

'A nurse!'

'Yes, what's wrong with that? It's an honest job.'

'Yes, an honest job as a slave. You'd have to wear those horrible nurse's shoes.'

'All you care about is appearances.'

'I'd still want you to be doing what suits you.'

'You don't know what my father is like. Saying that he's got a bad heart from worrying about money. He gets these little heart attacks when I go home for the weekend and even my mother says that they're put on. He says that no one loves him except Lassie.'

I shook Carl's hand off impatiently. 'I don't give two fucks about science, I want to do something I like before I get killed on the road. I read this book over the summer. *Wild Sargasso Sea.* All about the other Mrs Rochester. She was driven mad by *other people.*' I glared at Carl.

'Maeve, I've said I'm sorry.'

'And I'm going to read *Jane Eyre* again.'

'Jesus, you can read what you fucking like, I'm not stopping you.'

'I've failed,' I said.

'Maeve, you've hardly started your exams.'

'It's over, I'm getting away from my father.'

'I wouldn't exactly call nursing getting away.'

I was raging when I saw Tom and Josie sitting with Carl. 'I thought that you'd be on your own,' I whispered when Carl went up to get my drink.

'I couldn't tell them to go away!'

'Of course you could!'

'It's a free country, if they want to sit down at a table, I can't stop them.'

'You're always saying that it isn't a free country, that we should fight the system.'

'Josie and Tom aren't exactly *the system.* I thought if you came here you'd stop the dog's abuse.'

'You and Pierce, you want to get away with everything.'

'So there *was* something going on between you and Pierce,' Carl said, and it was nothing new. He said the exact same sentence about three times a week. Ger said it was like a soap opera and it drove me mental. 'Let him think it,' Ger said. 'It'll keep him on his toes.'

But I couldn't bear it. 'Listen here, you said you wouldn't say it any more. You know it's not true now and you're just saying it to try and distract me from your own viciousness.'

'Shhhh, here comes Myra!' said Carl and his face had coloured the way it always did when we argued about Pierce.

I wondered whether I should say hello, but Myra swept past me. She looked neater.

'Josie!' she cried.

'Didn't I tell you I'd be here?' Josie took a packet of Silk Cut out of her bag.

'What will you have?'

Josie seemed to be playing it a bit cool. She was drinking vodka and wearing high heels. Myra patted her hair and I realised what was different about her. She'd dyed her hair. It looked nice. Josie put a cigarette in her mouth. The cigarette looked very white next to her small brown hand. I noticed a huge rectangular ring with an emerald stone on her wedding finger. I was sure that it hadn't been there before.

Tom looked at me. 'Sorry about Carl.' I pretended I hadn't heard him but he went on as if I had answered him. 'No, I mean it. If I'd known you'd an exam, he never said.'

'Don't believe a word of it!' Josie exhaled a gush of grey smoke. 'He's only jealous of the two of you.

Although if you want my advice, don't hang around waiting. Go out yourself.'

'I could hardly go out the night before my exam.'

'There's always some excuse if you want to sit at home feeling sorry for yourself.'

Myra leaned over to me and asked in a false concerned voice, 'How's Geraldine?'

'She's fine,' I said.

'I'm glad,' Myra said and leaned back.

I couldn't figure out if Myra was being sarcastic or not. I bent down and fiddled with my boot. Stole a look at Pierce.

Pierce was still yellow and harsh-looking. He ignored the shouts of laughter that came from our table. Carl was talking to him.

I whispered to Tom, 'Were you doing wrecky last night?'

'I *never* do wrecky.'

'Is that a new drug?' Josie butted in.

'No, it's the name of a band,' Myra said. 'They've played in the city hall a couple of times.' Brazen as brass, and she hadn't a clue.

Carl sat down and I pretended to go to the loo. On the way back, I approached Pierce. I'd never seen Pierce with stubble before.

'Two packets of peanuts,' I said, hoping that he'd mention Ger first.

He didn't. 'Thirty pence, Maeve.'

'Ger wants to see you.'

'Oh does she now?' Pierce sounded savage. 'She deigns to speak to me?'

'Yes.'

'When the whole of Cork knows she's made a show of me.'

When I went back to my seat, I couldn't help looking at Myra. She looked triumphant.

'Look at Myra, how she's come on,' Josie whispered to me. 'She's been developing her own strength. Getting used to the idea.'

'You mean she knew that Ger was pregnant?'

Carl frowned at me, furiously. Too late.

'She's pregnant?' Josie's mouth opened. 'Where the bloody hell are my cigarettes?' Her small brown hand shook, making the red end of her cigarette look blurred.

· Twenty-eight ·

Pierce came round to the flat at two o'clock in the morning.

I woke up, heard Ger speaking to Pierce at the door. I woke Carl and I went out to the landing, shamelessly trying to hear.

'If he lays a hand on her,' Carl kept saying. I hoped for Carl's sake that Pierce wouldn't.

I was still groggy from the Benylin the night before and I tried to lie down on the landing.

Carl nearly lost his life. 'What are you doing? Get up!'

'I'm trying to get my ear to the ground.'

'We'll be fucking caught!'

'I'm so tired!'

'Go to bed!'

But I was afraid I'd miss something and part of me was dying for Pierce to do something wrong so that we could charge at him.

My teeth chattered and Carl held me against him, but the voices never rose above ocean-like murmurs caressing the floorboards under us. I bent down to chafe my feet which were gone numb and Carl told me I was the noisiest person he'd ever met. A chair scraped and footsteps came out to the hall. We fled into the bedroom. When the hall door shut quietly, we ran to the window and looked out. Pierce looked straight up at our window, his yellow gypsy face impassive in the dim lighting, and we shrank back, mortified. Not sure if he saw us or not.

'Fuck him anyway,' said Carl.

We went down the stairs to Ger who was drying up dishes in the kitchen.

'I'm glad he came, it's great to know I'm not missing anything,' said Ger, trying to be defiant with her eyes drowning in salt water.

'What's he going to do?'

'Oh, money,' said Ger. 'He said that I won't want for money. The scales have fallen from my eyes, that's all I can say. All he cares about is what Myra's going to think.'

'Well, I suppose you'd have to expect that!' Carl said.

It was terrible to witness her disappointment. What had she been hoping for? I don't think that she knew herself. We stayed up with her till five. I had to smoke to keep myself awake. Ger kept saying the scales were falling from her eyes. And all we could see were tears.

The next day Ger was angry. She walked around the flat, heavy and dangerous. Like an iceberg. At two o'clock in the afternoon she threw down *Moby Dick* and said she was going shopping. Said that she wanted me to give her a hand spending Pierce's money. She still had a load of the money which Pierce gave her for the abortion. She wasn't giving it back now.

I was afraid of what she might do on her own and Carl wasn't around to help me. All along Washington Street I ran beside her huge body, telling her to calm down. Feeling stupid because I knew that it was just the same as other people telling me to keep my head.

I nearly died when she turned into the Queen's Old Castle shopping centre.

'Everything is so dear!' I said.

Ger laughed like a maniac. 'The days of the Coal Quay are gone now, girl.'

The girls in Benetton didn't know what *we* were doing in there among the glass shelves and the immaculate wool. Ger was like an elephant dressed in black rags, I was wearing Carl's trousers rolled up and white tennis shoes with skulls and crossbones drawn all over them. I hadn't thought that I'd be leaving the house. The Benetton girls' eyes went up and down me like scanners. I kept telling myself that I didn't give a damn.

Ger bought a soft pink jumper. 'Do you remember those Spanish girls in Brixton?' she asked, squeezing the wool hard between her fingers.

The two girls in Benetton had sheets of shiny hair, just right for flicking back with their snowy pink-nailed hands. They did a lot of flicking and flinching as Ger mauled all the neatly folded jumpers.

I tried to be broadminded, reminding myself that they were only paid thirty-seven pounds a week. Claire had gone there for a summer job and that's what they offered her. For folding and folding the jumpers that people were constantly ransacking. But I still didn't like the way they looked at us. *Oh you with the grubby chimney-sweep paws, what are you doing touching our Holy Communion jumpers?*

Ger bought an emerald-green waistcoat, a scarlet cardigan and a white cotton blouse with crunchy romantic frills, two cute baby jumpers, orange and midnight blue.

Ger wanted to get me to buy something too, but I wouldn't, even though the colours nearly got to me, and the way the jumpers were piled up on the glass shelves like the mattresses in *The Princess and the Pea.*

I tried to get Ger home after that, but no, she wanted to go to Sue Ellen's where it cost an arm and a leg for a toasted sandwich.

'I've still got rakes left.' She opened her pencil case, recklessly showing off the rolls of navy-blue notes.

I gave in. The smell of food was getting to me and I thought things weren't too bad when we were sitting down with our toasted sandwiches, nice little delicate mounds of coleslaw and thin chips on the side.

'Ye fucking aristocrats!' We heard Murphy's voice. 'What are ye doing in here?'

'What are *you* doing here?'

'I only came in to go to the jacks. Never again, boy! The place is full of fucking steamers.'

Murphy sat down with us and I was proud of the attention he was getting from the shoppers all around. 'Steamers' was a Cork City word for gay men. Murphy was saying he reckoned it came about because of the turkish baths they had in Cork years ago. He did Ger a power of good, especially the way he didn't stare at her stomach. Or *not* look at it either.

When Murphy left, Ger promised she'd go home if we had one more coffee. She seemed to have calmed down. I was in the queue when I saw Myra and Josie coming into Sue Ellen's with bags and bags of shopping. Pierce didn't know what an awful lot of business he was giving to clothes shops that day.

There was nowhere to hide. I tried to catch Ger's eye but her head was bent over the table. Josie saw us and tried to turn Myra back. When Ger looked up and saw Myra, she tried squeeze out from behind the table.

There was another exit. She would have got away if her stomach hadn't got jammed behind the table. Everyone turned to look at her. Myra too. At last Ger managed to free herself. Myra looked from Ger's red dishevelled face to her stomach and screamed. The Benetton girls ran out from their shop to look at us. The woman at the cash desk was shouting *your coffees love* in a very unloving voice. But I didn't care. I left the coffee with her. I ran to gather the bags, squeezing past Myra who was blocking my path. Josie was shaking her head.

'And to think of me, as pure as the driven snow, and I can't have children,' Myra was saying to some woman who kept lifting the *Cork Examiner* higher and nearer to her face. Trying to pretend Myra wasn't there.

Ger had already fled with one of the Benetton bags and I caught up with her at the back entrance of the shopping centre. Ger cursed Pierce from a height, and halfway home started laughing and jeering about Myra. I supposed that she couldn't help it but it was awful bitter stuff.

'I really like that emerald-green jumper you got,' I said.

'Do you think am I too sallow for it?'

'It's the gear knock,' I said, and went on like a shot, talking about the mattresses in *The Princess and the Pea*. I thought Ger would think I was a right baby, but apparently fairy tales were a fine thing to talk about.

We were laughing at some stupid joke I made when Myra passed by in a taxi. She didn't see us but Josie did. Later Josie said that she'd never seen anything so callous as the way we were laughing. She blamed us for her going back on the drink.

· *Twenty-nine* ·

The afternoon I finished my exams, Murphy dropped by. No T-shirt, a pair of baggy pinstripe trousers and sneakers painted luminous pink. Murphy was fierce clothes-conscious. Jimmy Barry said he didn't give a fuck about that. Jimmy Barry said that he was just a gurrier from the North Side. Denied that he ever said he was a punk.

'I'm just an animal!' he said, after Best's defection. One of the bones in his hand was broken where he'd punched the wall. The plaster was in the shape of a fingerless mitten and his stubby hard fingers stuck out at the end, trapped and helpless-looking.

'I don't go round reading philosophy and saying it's fucking absurd. I don't have time for that, boy!'

Carl agreed. 'The idea of punk is *no* fucking rules.' And added carefully, 'Not that I'm a punk.'

'Or a mod either, strictly speaking like!' Jimmy said. Carl didn't look pleased when he said *that.*

Murphy asked us were we definitely jagging and I told him straight out that I was having none of Carl's advances while he was still into wrecky.

'Are you still into that?' Murphy asked, surprised. 'I've given all that up. Bad for the old heart, boy. Ruins the clothes. I'm writing a play now.'

'About what?' I asked, while Carl stood by the record player chewing his lip.

'Just an existential working-class play.'

'Oh, yeah?' said Carl.

Murphy looked a bit embarrassed. 'Throw on a bit of music there.'

Carl bent down looking through the records. 'Jesus, look, here's Tom's Revilos album.'

'Throw it on, throw it on,' Murphy said and grabbed my hand. Then Carl leaped in and we were going berserk, shaking our hips, when I thought that I saw a face pressed against the kitchen window. An old man with white hair. At first I thought that it was Mr Sheehan, the landlord. I stopped dancing. I shouted at Murphy and Carl but they couldn't hear me. The kitchen door opened tentatively. The music stopped for a few split seconds after each chorus. Murphy shrieked into the silence.

'Daddy!' I said. I went over to the record player and turned it off.

He didn't wait two seconds. 'I knew you were doing nothing, but I never thought you'd sink as low as this.'

I opened my mouth but nothing came. There was a drone in my ears as if everything was happening very far away. I heard the front door slam and Ger's slow footsteps. Carl leaned up against the table and crossed his legs. Murphy stood with his hands on his hips the way he always stood when he was expecting a scrap.

I felt bad about all the things I'd said to Carl about my father. He wasn't really that bad. He was an old man, for god's sake.

'Bootboys,' my father started. He was only ten years behind in his terminology which wasn't bad for him. He stopped when Ger opened the door. My father's pink mouth hung open as his eyes swept over Ger's stomach. 'The lowest of the low,' he said, and he kept looking at Ger as if she was scum. 'Is this what my money is supporting? A den of iniquity. Vandals,' he said, looking at Carl and Murphy.

I couldn't bear the way he was looking at Ger. 'Daddy, you know that I earned my own money in London.'

'Sure, you'd me fooled into thinking you'd studied this time.'

It was so unfair. 'I *have* studied, but I'm giving it up now.'

'Oh a drop-out now is it?'

'Yes, I'm a drop-out, I'm going to be a nurse.'

'Oh, I'd say they'd love you.' I hated the way he spoke. The sarcasm. Always directed at myself and my mother, never pointed in the right direction. 'Oh, I'd say they'd love you, the nuns above in the Bons. Oh, you're right up their alley with your black eyes and your electrocuted hair.' My father's face was tinged with purple. I thought, any minute he's going to get the bloody fatal heart attack. Just my luck.

'I suppose you'll give her a reference.' My father jerked his thumb at Murphy. 'Who is this Teddy Boy?' Oh god, the way he spoke! His flat country accent.

Murphy didn't take his hands off his hips for a minute. 'I'm her bit of rough,' he said, and blinked his eyes innocently. His whole body screaming *I'm just dying for a scrap!*

My father's eyes widened, he clenched his fists. I could see that he was both afraid and stubborn. He looked at Carl as if daring him to say something.

'I'm bringing you home now,' my father said. 'I told you from day one you were going to fail.'

'Daddy, I can't come, don't get upset. Your heart,' I added foolishly, knowing that I'd told everyone about

206

his pretend heart attacks. And I hadn't just *told* them, I'd demonstrated. Only last week I'd staggered around the table with my hand inside my shirt, clutching my heart, *oh Helen go easy with the money when I'm gone will you?* And Ger and Carl falling around the place. I didn't dare look at them now.

'If your poor mother was here, and she was going to come you know!'

'I can't go back.'

'Starve then.'

'I'm getting a job,' I said. 'I'm not cut out for conventional life!'

''Twas far from conventional life you were reared,' my father shouted.

'You wouldn't know anything about it, would you?' Carl said. 'With your twenty-five first-cousins priests and your uncle Lord Abbot of Glenstall Abbey?'

'Mocking your family, telling your business to the tramps on the street. Oh what a daughter! What a repayment!'

I'd been feeling sorry for him, I'd been going to walk him to the gate until he mentioned repayment.

'Is that all you can think about? Returns for your investments. How could you think of getting anything when you buried me?' Wasn't there something in the gospel about burying talents?

My father stared at me disbelievingly. I watched his familiar hand creeping across his shirt to his heart getting ready to simulate an attack. I hated the little white hairs on his knuckles.

'And don't have one of your stupid heart attacks in my flat!'

My father's hand stopped halfway across his chest. He dived across the table, the wood creaking under his weight. He got his fist under my chin. 'I'll break your bloody face!'

Carl and Murphy caught him and held him back. My father's pinky purple face twisted and scowling at me. I shook from head to foot. *You'll be old some day!*

He was too old, it shouldn't have happened like this.

'You'll rue the day you abused your father,' he said. 'I won't,' I shouted.

But I was afraid that I would. The Fourth Commandment and everything. *You'll have no luck for it*, my mother would say, any time I tried to stand up to him before. And the way he brought up his fists so quick. When I was tiny, up against the marble fireplace in the dining room.

His hair was ruffled at the back, there were creases across his good suit. At the door he looked back at me. I was sure that he was going to say something but he just breathed faster as if he'd decided he was going to have that heart attack after all. Make me pay for it. I closed my eyes and when I opened them he was gone.

I stood bent over for a few seconds. I could hear his heavy footsteps going out to the hall door. I thought that I was going to vomit. I gave a tiny retch and stood up.

'You were great,' Carl said.

'Now you know why I hate fucking violence,' I said, sitting down. I crossed my leg. My foot was wobbling everywhere, I had the shakes so bad. I uncrossed my legs again and sat with my fists jammed firmly on my knees.

'You're as white as a sheet,' Ger said.

'Get her a drink,' Murphy said, but we never had

any spare drink in the flat. That was luxury. Everything we had was consumed on the spot apart from tea. Ger made some.

'He was a right bastard,' Murphy said. 'Jesus, I never knew about the twenty-five first-cousin priests. Ye're a mad family!'

'He is mad,' I said, shuddering. 'I hated the way he was looking at Ger.'

While I was drinking my tea, my resolve was failing. 'I shouldn't have treated him like that, it was awful.'

'He was looking for it,' Murphy said.

'He was horrible,' Ger said.

'I don't think he realizes it,' I said.

'Fuck him,' Carl said, his thin mouth looking disgusted.

'Hey, come here to me! What's this about you becoming a nurse?' Murphy asked.

'Oh nothing, it was just an idea I had. I'd like to be something definite.'

'But you don't know what you want,' Ger said. 'The last thing you should be doing is rushing into another job.'

'I thought nursing was kind of classless.'

'Classless!' roared Murphy. 'Jesus, you think it's bad out here in the world. You should go into a hospital and experience the hierarchy. It's fucking murder.'

He waved Carl to one side with his naked, muscly arm. 'Maeve, student nurses have to sell their souls. Those cat uniforms! Those fucking shoes! That's not for you, Maeve.'

'Nurses themselves are fine, though,' Ger said. 'I've a cousin a nurse, she's really sound.'

'I've an aunt a nurse,' Carl said. 'She's really brilliant at doing bandages. Smokes like a trooper. I think she takes drugs as well. It's just the fucking system that's cat.'

'It's true for Ger anyway,' Carl went on. 'You can't rush into another thing, what if you don't like it!' He sat on the table and crossed his legs again and said, 'You're right about the nurses' shoes, Murphy.' Carl turned back to me. 'Fucking hell, I'd divorce you if you got into a pair of those.' And I was thinking, oh his beautiful red hair, I'll never get a young Henry the Eighth again!

I burst into tears. 'I'll divorce *you* if you don't stop the fucking violence.'

Carl took me to see *Chariots of Fire* at the Capitol to cheer me up. We thought that it was full of elitism.

'You were right to stand up to him. He was treating you like shit.'

'I bet you'd feel the same if it was your father.'

'I wish I could tell him to fuck off,' Carl said.

'I thought that you'd have done it ages ago!'

'No, I can't, I need the financial support.'

'If he found out about the wrecky, would he keep giving you financial support?'

Carl was quiet for a bit, then said, 'Look, Maeve, I haven't done any wrecky since before the exams. The way you went on about it just annoyed me. I suppose I'm a mule sometimes. I was jealous of Pierce and I didn't want to be giving in to you.'

'You can't have wanted sex that much, and I can't believe you're still talking about Pierce.'

'I didn't need you to tell me that wrecky's fucking meaningless, and look at Best. Jesus, a middle-class thug. Now it seems a bit like being spoilt or something. I was so angry though, the way the world is so fucking unfair. Best really sickened me. The way he played around for a while. He said that Jimmy Barry could be the bass guitarist and then he never bothered forming the rest of the band. I know Jimmy was gutted, though he never let on. It was a big thing to him you know. When does he ever get a chance to do something like that?'

'I forgot about that band,' I said, casting my mind back. It seemed like another age now. The time before we went to London.

Carl went on, 'Jimmy Barry and Murphy are worth ten of Best. You don't realise it, they act so cheerful, but they have fucking hard lives. Have you ever been up to Mayfield? Bleak. Blocks of flats and lines of washing. The children's faces. The women with piles of children, you wouldn't know what age they were.'

'Murphy seems to manage okay.'

'It's all a front!' Carl said.

We were passing Curtains and Carl wanted to go in.

'Alright, but I'm not talking to Pierce,' I said. 'I don't like his attitude to Ger.'

I gave Carl fifty-five pence for my pint of cider and sat in the corner. Thinking. About Jimmy Barry and Murphy and bleakness. How stupid I was to be thinking about nursing. Panicking because I hadn't got a place somewhere. Rushing into another mistake. Another institution.

'Pierce is really jaundiced-looking,' I said when Carl sat down with our drinks. 'I hope he's going through hell.'

'Well, he was in a no-win situation,' Carl said.

'That's not very loyal to Ger,' I said, indignantly.

'I'm only rising you,' Carl said and put his hand on my leg. 'I mean it about giving up wrecky and all that kind of thing. I'd hate to see you looking at me the way you looked at your father. When he had his fist against your throat.'

'Well, you never did anything to *me!*'

'I know, but you hate it and I know it's stupid.'

'I was so ashamed of my father in front of you.'

'It's not your fault,' Carl said. 'You should meet mine. He's got an English accent and a soft handshake.'

'Are you a Protestant?' I asked, curious when he mentioned the English accent.

'I am, yeah. Do you mind?'

'No, no, god what do you think I am?' I said, hoping that I hadn't said anything stupid about Protestants.

Pierce kept trying to nod at me but I ignored him. Finally he came over to the table. I thought that there was going to be some kind of showdown and then he said that Myra wanted to see me. I got up straight away.

'Not now,' Pierce said hastily, as if he was half afraid of me. 'Come in some afternoon during the week.'

'What was all that about? Do you think it's about Ger?'

'He's only dying to get his hands on you again,' Carl said.

'Don't start again please,' I said.

And Carl asked me did I know that half the girls in college were mad about Pierce now. Ger had given Pierce notoriety. People looked at him differently these days. I said that I was looking at him differently these days, thinking what a yellow-livered bastard he was coming down again to Ger and abusing her, frightening her in her own flat. Just because he left it too late to tell Myra.

'You were seen laughing in Washington Street,' he shouted at Ger.

'Am I supposed to be in mourning?' Ger shouted back. Ger said she felt like really showing him what making a show was. She felt like landing the baby in over the counter when it was born and saying here's your bastard.

'Well, thank your stars it wasn't *you* that he got pregnant,' Carl said.

I got drunk very fast. Carl couldn't get a word in, I was talking so quickly. I said that now that I'd told my father to fuck off, maybe I was a bit of a punk after all. Punk was the ultimate way of saying no and I was saying no to college as well. I was going to read all the things I wanted to read. The books that Murphy and Ger read. And maybe when I liked something as much as Ger liked English then I might, just might, study something again. I said that Murphy was my example of an alternative person and Carl said that Murphy would have given his two eyes to have gone to college. I thought that that was awful sad because Murphy was away better than the usual college types.

'What did Best go doing an engineering degree for if he was going into the family business?' I said.

'Status,' said Carl and bought more drink.

We were kissing by the end of the night, all squashed up in the corner. Carl's long legs were thrown over mine. It was even more thrilling now that I knew Carl was a Protestant. Like wearing a swastika armband.

When we got back to the flat, I let Carl take my bra off. His hands were barely warm and very smooth, his lips were cold. I could smell cider the whole time.

Sometimes in old black-and-white films a circle forms around a kissing couple. The couple and the circle get smaller until they finally disappear into a white dot and the credits go up. Carl and I were right in the middle of the little white dot.

I was afraid that it might be sordid, that his body would be too white or too red-haired, but it wasn't a bit like that.

It was like the last few seconds before you get an injection. It hurt, but I didn't say anything – I was trying to be nice. Then the warmth came. We were up all night and used all the contraceptives that Carl had brought in the brown paper bag from the illegal family planning clinic in Tuckey Street. I went down there with him the next day. It was great, we were like members of the French Resistance. Secret and righteous. Clandestine. I kept thinking, I've had *sex*.

· *Thirty* ·

Ger got very weepy about the baby. She kept saying
that she was strong enough and that she would carry
on regardless in all weather, but why was life so unfair.
That Fate was a hard bastard. I thought that Fate was
a woman. Or three women. I'd been reading. Getting
knowledgeable myself. But I said nothing to Ger of
course. She got the loveliest letter from her mother
and nearly cracked up. Handed it over to me as if it
was the sheriff's notice my father was always talking
about.

Dun Mhuire,
Cooltown,
Co. Waterford.

16th September

Dear Geraldine,
I am so sorry and right in the middle of your
important studies. But remember that in some ways I
have been in the same boat (more or less alone) six
times and I have never regretted it. I have loved every
one of my little girls.
I have answered an advertisement in the Cork Examiner offering an unfurnished house for rent in St
Luke's. It sounds lovely just beside the church, old,

215

very big. The man said that it is hard to rent unfurnished in Cork City with all the students. That's why it is so cheap. We are moving in at the end of September. They say I will have no trouble getting dressmaking work. I already have the name of someone who wants curtains made.

You're a brave little girl. It will be like old times with us all together helping out. You'll get your degree, I owe you that much.

Your Loving Mum

P.S. The girls send their love. Teresa's knitting a pair of bootees already!

Ger threw herself around. I was afraid that she'd go into premature labour.

'Is she up for a canonisation or what? I can't bear it! I bet she wouldn't be like that if I'd phoned her straight away, she has a temper. She'd like to pretend that she hasn't.'

'God, she's brilliant. I don't care. Moving to Cork like that,' I said, thinking about my parents and their varicose vein competitions.

'She hates Waterford, she was only dying to get out of it.' Ger had taken up biting her nails. The crescent of a bitten-off piece hung off her cheek. 'I don't want to live with them all again. I don't want to go to mass, I'll be right back to square one.'

'But, you need help,' I said. I couldn't help feeling relieved that someone else was leaping into the fray. Worried about how the baby was going to affect me. Selfish.

Ger sulked and bit her nails even more, leaning her elbows on her stomach as if it was a shelf.

Who were the real villains? Parents or children?

Fairy tales moved all the blame on top of the poor old stepmothers with the punky hairstyles. Although some fairy tales did go for the jugular. The Fourth Commandment must have been getting to them too. Or maybe someone had to make up the Fourth Commandment to keep the boot down on the crowd who were making up the fairy tales.

Jack's nagging mother in *Jack and the Beanstalk*. The parents in *Hansel and Gretel. Tom Thumb*, his parents *sold* him. In all three stories the parents were looking for money. And who were always saying that money isn't everything? My father talking to Father Cashman, *sure I'm always saying to Maeve what good is it? You can't take it to the grave with you.* My mother, her wardrobe bulging with bags of unmentionable treasure from Richard Allen's. *Never get hung up on money, Maeve. Don't turn out like your father.*

Later I had a bit of a revelation. Ger was asleep and I woke her up.

'You know the way your mother was paranoid about letters getting intercepted and never put anything more than small talk in a letter?'

'Yes?'

'Well don't you see she's written about your baby in the letter. You can't get anything more delicate or important than that.'

Ger scowled. 'And you woke me up to tell me that!' Furious that I'd managed to think up more good about her mother. Turned her back and closed her eyes. 'If my sleep is broken I won't be responsible for my actions.'

Ger had to pull herself out of it when Claire called round. Claire had some kind of a baby's blanket she'd found in her mother's junk room. A faded lemon and blue plaid. Ger was worried it might be a souvenir, something with sentimental value. Claire said that it wasn't, but I had the impression she'd taken it without asking her mother.

Claire was a lot quieter. She'd given up on the Charlie's Angels hair. She had a flat ponytail pulled back from her face, her eyes looked luminous. Soulful. Like a real princess. She said that she didn't have giggling problems any more. This autumn she was going to begin dissecting real human bodies. She didn't laugh about it. I wondered if she was thinking about Fred's mossy grave. I was. Thinking just as well that he hadn't donated his body to medicine or he might have turned up on her dissection table.

We were sitting around drinking coffee and talking about the baby and Claire was doing some trick with a ring and a piece of string to work out the sex of it, when we heard the singing.

The violets were scenting the woods, no-ra
Displaying their charms to the bees
When I first said I loved only you, no-ra
And you said you loved only me.

'What is it?' asked Claire. I could swear that there was the ghost of a smile around her lips.

'It's Mr Sheehan the landlord,' said Ger, and jumped up. 'Oh Jesus, he's going to throw me out!'

The singing came closer and louder like a zombie's footsteps.

The chestnuts bloom gleams through the glade, no-ra

The robin sang out from every tree
When I first said I loved only you, no-ra
And you said you loved only me.

We all tried to look serious. Claire folded her arms, I
started writing in an A4 pad and Ger took up *Moby
Dick.* Mr Sheehan knocked and I called out, 'Come in,
Mr Sheehan.'

'How did you know I was here?' he said.

'You always sing my favourite song,' I said, going too
far as usual. Ger gave a snort.

He was wearing a straw-coloured toupée plonked
on top of his grey hair. I could feel a laugh coming on.
Claire's smile was getting less ghostly.

He gave a quick look at Ger, but he didn't seem to
register anything.

'I'm here about a a ah.' He broke off, and we knew
that he'd noticed Ger's stomach. Ger was giving little
titters.

'I'm here about the business of of of.' He broke off
again and I was holding the A4 pad over my mouth.

'I'm here about the situation of of of . . .' I was going
to say the word 'pregnancy' for him but he finished
off, 'the situation of lolly!' His tongue rolled right out
of his mouth like a red carpet when he said the word
'lolly'.

That was the end of us. I hung over the side of the
chair gasping for air, Ger laughed into his face and
Claire was kicking her legs as if she was being tickled.

Mr Sheehan stared at us with a confused red face.
'Is it the way you haven't got any lolly?' His tongue
rolled out again and we shook our heads. The table
could hardly bear the weight of our struggles. It began
to creak as we leaned against it.

'Mind the table, girls!' He was half smiling, half pretending that he was in on the joke too.

'It's a serious thing.' He was getting mad. 'Twenty-four pounds. I could get the guards on ye.'

Ger got up and staggered over to her basket and took out a pencil case. Claire was wiping her eyes with a handkerchief. Ger took out an almighty roll of twenty-pound notes. She was still carrying around the rest of the money that Pierce had given her for the abortion.

Mr Sheehan cheered up but he still looked uncomfortable. 'Ye're in good form today, is the studying going well?'

Claire burst out again, her eyes shining with unshed tears.

'I hope ye're not on drugs,' he said then. 'That's an awful lot of money to be carrying around in a pencil case.'

'But who'd suspect me of being that rich?' Ger said.

'No one,' he said. 'Not in those rags,' he added, getting a bit of revenge.

'We don't believe in outer show,' I said to him.

'You don't need to tell me.' He was still a bit mad with us, but he began edging towards the door. He hadn't said anything about Ger having a baby.

Ger went over and stood right next to him. We were all staring at her stomach.

'Look, girleen, I've seen it all before. As long as you pay your rent you can stay here.' His hand was impatient on the door.

I could see that Ger was about to thank him when a mean expression came over his face. 'Well, I've only got the greatest pity for you! Really, I wouldn't want to be in your situation if I got Ireland free in the morning.'

Ger stared at him for a moment, then said, 'Actually I'd better tell you that I'll be moving out at the end of September. Moving in with my mother who's just written me a lovely letter.'

'Lovely letter is it?' said Mr Sheehan.

'Yes,' I said. 'I'm moving too. Do you know that the whole of college thinks this flat is haunted? I hope you'll be able to replace us.'

'Don't be hasty now. Haunted! Sure ye young girls have great imagination.'

'Well, I'm not scared at all, the knocking has stopped. I'm just telling you what they're saying round college.'

'Knocking, for god's sake, that's the central heating next door.'

'It isn't the central heating in here anyway, that's for sure. It's been like the North Pole all winter.'

'That's enough,' Ger said to me. 'Goodbye, Mr Sheehan.'

'There's no need to move you know, I'm a charitable man.'

'You heard Maeve, Mr Sheehan,' Claire piped up, without the trace of a giggle. 'Ger couldn't possibly have her baby living in these conditions.'

'What conditions? 'Tis all imagination. Wasn't I up and down to that attic all winter with sheets of asbestos.'

'Asbestos did you say? Are you aware of the dangers?' Claire got up from her chair and approached him.

'Well, well, well, that's it I suppose. If you have to go ye have to go.' Mr Sheehan was almost running to the door.

'What about the asbestos?' Claire called after his retreating figure, just to see him going faster. There was no lingering to sing about violet-scented woods in the hallway this time. He was in his car and away very quick.

'Oh, *you* are going to make a very good doctor,' Ger said, half sarcastic, but you could see that she admired Claire.

· *Thirty-one* ·

I went to see Myra. I had to keep cool out of loyalty
to Ger, but the curiosity was killing me.

'Pierce said you wanted to see me.'

'Well, I did. I like you, you know.'

'Thanks,' I said, doubtfully.

'I heard you're giving up college.'

'Yes.'

'What are you going to do?'

'I don't know,' I said, wondering what all this had
to do with Ger and Ger's baby.

'Well, you're going to need money and we could do
with some help. Pierce is fierce mean but I'll make
him pay you well.'

'Gee, thanks but I wouldn't know how to fill a pint
or anything.'

'Nonsense, come in under the counter and I'll show
you straight away.'

Myra said that she had learned if you did something
well it made life a lot more bearable. As if I was suicidal
or something. I kept thinking, money. My own money.

I wondered why I'd ever thought that she was mad,
and for a moment her untidy ponytail looked carelessly romantic as she showed me how to hold the
glass sideways and fill slowly, giving the Guinness plenty

of time to rest along the way. Waiting each time for the golden-brown particles to drift into black until I'd filled three beautiful pints the colour of jet, with one quarter of an inch of cream, slightly rounded at the top of each glass.

'What are you going to do with them now?' I asked. 'Isn't it a terrible waste?'

'This is training,' said Myra and suggested that we sit down and drink them if I was so worried. I said Ger was waiting for me. 'She'll be getting a big cheque from Pierce soon,' Myra said. 'I'll be seeing to that.'

Two men came in as I was leaving. 'How's that for service!' said Myra, landing the pints in front of them. 'That's one pound twenty-two please.'

We were eating pears the day my exam results came out. Ger had got them cheap because they were going off. Yellow-brown mottled skin fell in snakes onto an old blue plate while Ger piled whitish chunks into a bowl.

Carl came round with a bag of chocolate saws. He was acting a bit tense.

'Lovely,' he said when I offered him the bowl, and took a slithery piece in his hand.

I read a bit from *Jane Eyre* to him. 'Listen to this!' Some of the pages were hanging out. One fluttered to the floor as I found the place I was looking for.

I know no weariness of my Edward's society: he knows none of mine, any more than we each do of the pulsation of the heart that beats in our separate bosoms.

Carl and I were getting a flat together. I was sure that he would get the connection.

'You must be near the end,' Carl said, looking a bit embarrassed. I kept getting the impression he was trying to make signs to Ger behind my back.

'Stop fooling around,' I said.

'The exam results are out,' Carl said quickly, the piece of pear bulging in his cheek.

I could have said that I didn't care until my tongue dropped out of my mouth, but hope really does spring eternal. I had to get a chair and sit down. *Jane Eyre* fell under the table.

'Well?' I said.

'Are you ready to go up?' Carl was playing with the brown bag as he spoke.

'No, no, I can't!'

'Maeve, the sooner you're out of your misery,' Ger said.

'Yeah, the sooner I find out that I've failed.' I turned to Carl. 'You were up there, why didn't you look them up?'

'I thought that you'd want to look yourself. That's what you said yesterday.' Carl ran his hand through his new square-looking crew cut.

'And that was before, when I was brave.'

'You're still brave.' Ger put down her knife. 'Come on, Maeve, I'll get your coat.' She went into the bedroom and came back with my donkey jacket. 'I can't face that stone arch, having to look for my name in front of everyone!'

It wasn't easy. A crowd of loud engineers blocked the notice board. Shouting and cheering. It looked like they'd all passed.

A cold wind cut through the arch. I shivered behind Carl as he pushed his way through the engineers. I waited for him to call out, but he said nothing, his red head looking this way and that, peering up and down the columns.

Finally, the engineers went off, running. Talking

225

about pints and next year. I was able to get a look at the notice board. Like Carl, I kept looking up and down the lists.

There was nothing. No 'Maeve Cronin' no matter how hard we looked. I buttoned my jacket up and forced my hands savagely into my pockets. Carl put his arm around me.

'Look, you didn't want science anyway, you said.'

'I'd like to have had a bloody choice about it.'

'There's an N. Cronin there.'

'I know, I kept looking at it. Hoping. But it's Norma Cronin, she was repeating as well. She used to go to the same physics grind. They'd never make a mistake like that.'

Carl squeezed my arm. 'Let's go for a drink.'

I didn't move. My eyes were fixed to the notice board. 'It's awful not being able to find my name. Like being written out of my life or something.'

'It's a stupid way of doing the results, they should post them to you.'

'But then I'd hate the postman!'

My eyes began to water. 'I'd better go before I make a show of myself.'

'There isn't anyone else around, you know,' Carl said. 'Except for those engineer eedjits. They're probably all off consoling themselves.'

'N. Cronin isn't consoling herself,' I pointed out, and took my hand out of my pocket to stab a cold red finger at the notice board. 'And all those engineers passed, for god's sake. I heard them. I'm not deaf.'

Pierce's language had got worse. Fuck this and fuck that.

'Well, did you get the results yet?' Pierce asked in a gloomy voice.

Carl shook his head.

'Don't talk to me about fucking results,' Pierce said to Carl. 'I've been through the whole fucking caboodle with Myra. In fact, you know, she's never been right since.'

'He's saying that I'm going to end up like Myra,' I whispered despairingly to Carl.

'Speak up,' Pierce told me. 'It's rude to whisper. That's what happened to Myra. She started whispering and then she wouldn't leave the house. Knotting into herself.'

I took a huge gulp from Carl's pint of cider.

'Drinking will only make you worse,' Pierce told me.

'Will you leave her alone!' Carl raised his voice.

'I'm sorry,' Pierce said. And moved to the other end of the bar to turn on the television. My future employer, and we were abusing him. We knew we could do it because of what he'd done to Ger.

We sat at a table. A video came on. The Specials. *This town is coming like a ghost town. Aw aw.* Oh bittersweet! I couldn't help enjoying it. Then the engineers struck up in the lounge. *We are the engineers, we are the best. We are the engineers, and fuck all the rest.*

'Do you feel as stupid as that?' Carl said and I had to admit that I didn't.

And yet I still hated the fact that I failed my exams. I'd have to face all the other students when I was working behind the bar. *How will I face the public?* my mother used to say when my father wouldn't let her buy a new suit for Easter Sunday. She had the suit at the back of the wardrobe already but she couldn't bring it out.

Pierce gave us free drink for the rest of the evening and I said that we'd never have known he was bad if he hadn't got involved with Ger. Carl said that I was only waiting to get involved with Pierce myself once Myra was gone off to St Anne's for her annual nervous breakdown.

We are the engineers, we are the best, we are the engineers, and fuck all the rest.

Carl said it was very punky to fail. To be a successful punk you had to fail, that's why the Pistols didn't last. Failure was built into them.

I suppose I'd known it was coming really. Science had been a glass mountain that I hadn't really wanted to climb. It was a relief when I could give up floundering. Sliding around.

· *Thirty-two* ·

We had arrived in college, pretending that we'd mush-
roomed out of the ground, totally free of any parental
links. We ended up discussing our parents all the time.
Especially after what Murphy called the big schmozzel
with my father. Even Jimmy Barry and Murphy. People
butted in and interrupted. Everyone wanted to have
the worst story. Just like home.

Murphy's mother was a gambling alcoholic claustro-
phobic, but Jimmy Barry's father beat his mother every
day for going off with a tinker while he was away in
the merchant navy. She had to wear sunglasses the
whole time. Jimmy Barry got beaten twice a day for
being the offspring of the alleged affair. The savage
twist to the story was that Jimmy had a twin sister and
the father never beat her. He said that she really *was*
his child. Apparently you can have twins by two
different fathers. Mr Barry had read up on it.

When Jimmy Barry was gone I said that we'd have to
be nicer to Jimmy Barry. Ger wanted to know if I was the
blindest person she'd ever met. That Jimmy Barry
couldn't tell the truth to save his life and the truth about
Jimmy was probably far worse and not a bit romantic.

Murphy did the best though, because his plays about
families were brilliant. He joined a writers group and

they all idolized him. Wishing that they were working-class and hadn't done repressive degrees in English. *And all that wonderful material from Mayfield!* We got a bit sick of him, because he got attached to his groupies and they never let us slag him.

Ger got very annoyed with us slating our parents all the time. Even Tom, who was her right-hand man, helping her with the shopping, bringing her records and everything. She couldn't get enough of blues stuff. No Good Men, Wasted Life, Blue Spirits, Graveyards, Cemeteries, Worn Out Papas and more No Good Men.

'Tom complains the whole time about his mother drinking. I'm going to be a mother soon. Is this the way my child is going to talk about me? The child that's growing up and out every bloody way inside me. The child that's squashing all the air out of my lungs?'

Carl told her that Tom was more fool to be indulging her with the blues, and I told him to fuck off.

That winter was hard enough, moving in with Carl and wanting the flat clean and Carl useless sometimes. Working in Curtains was hard, too, but then I'd get my money and buy cushions and rugs and stuff. If Carl was studying I'd draw in my secret copybook.

My mother's letter went astray for a while after I moved, and then someone brought it in to Curtains.

Lake View,
Rathpeak,
Co. Limerick

September

Dear Maeve,

Your father is very upset. Can you find it in your heart to ring and apologize? I didn't want to put this bit in, but your father insisted. If you get a job could you send a bit home to pay for your fees at least?

If your father said anything bad, you know he didn't mean it. He's very upset.

Please ring.

With Good Luck in the exams,

Your Loving Mum

Myra drummed it in to me that she didn't want me to turn out like she did. It was one thing that Pierce and herself agreed on. That I was the image of Myra when she was young. Mentally, physically, the whole caboodle. And I couldn't complain, they were so good to me.

Every now and then Pierce took me to one side and gave me extra money for Ger. Said that he had to pretend to be really mean about Ger's baby so that Myra would think all the generosity was coming from herself.

And Myra talked about Ger too. 'I know she's moving in with her mother, but don't desert her. Don't ever desert your girlfriends.'

'Didn't Josie desert you a bit?'

'No, she has to go back to her teaching and she was very good to me. Besides,' Myra gave me a proud look, 'I try to keep a low profile, the school authorities mightn't be pleased to know that she's hanging around with me.'

I didn't think that there was much fear of that since we hadn't seen Josie for months.

'I was arrested once, you know.' Myra took the elastic band off her ponytail and shook her hair out over her shoulders.

'Arrested for what?'

'Carrying explosives.'

'*No!*'

'Oh yes, you were probably too young to remember the time of the bombing of the British Embassy. We were on a march and it was just petrol bombs. Everyone was doing it, even old-age pensioners. I never got to it. The bloody guards picked me up a mile off. I was just like you, useless at camouflage.'

'Were you in the IRA?'

'No, no. I was a Trotskyite after I failed my exams. The bombing of the British Embassy was just a kind of a general blow for freedom. Anyone who was passing pitched in. There was even a young banker who thought he wouldn't be seen and he got caught rotten on the front page of the *Irish Independent*. I'd say that was the end of *him* handing out loans to people.'

'Was being arrested awful?'

'I expected to get beaten up and everything, standing up for my revolutionary principles, but the sergeant decided I was an innocent led astray. *Don't be tiring me out with your blackguarding,* he said when I was making my speech. Just locked me up and left me for a couple of hours. Let me go without pressing charges. *I wouldn't like to upset your daddy.*'

'He didn't know your daddy?'

'Well, he did actually.' Myra looked ashamed and began to gather her hair back into the ponytail. 'My father was a super in Kerry and the worst bit was being so relieved about it. I hated myself for ages afterwards and then I became an anarchist.'

Myra's kind of anarchy was different from the Sex Pistols. It wasn't just chaos. Apparently there were some real ones who were organized. They had a magazine called *Freedom.* They believed in a harmonious society in which government was abolished as totally unnecessary. They were peaceful, against all the

232

nuclear stuff and technology and were into making their own things. Carl said they were just a heap of hippies really, but he liked to stay up late chatting to Myra about them.

The more we talked, the more I read. Anarchy was really weird and brilliant and it had loads of meanings. Shelley's *Song of Anarchy* said that the dictator types like Castlereagh were the anarchists, spreading violence and chaos, keeping the true authority away from the people.

Pierce looked sad sometimes and I exaggerated this to Ger to keep her spirits up. Myra kept telling him what a vicious character he was, deserting Ger. Her peaceful anarchist principles were not applied to Pierce. That's what marriage was all about, Carl said, as if I was thinking about such a thing.

'As if she'd let me go,' Pierce said with clenched fists in the gloomy barrel house when he was helping me to change a barrel of Murphy's.

At first I thought that they should really get a divorce or something. I thought couples stayed together because of the children and they had none, unless you counted Myra's nerves and Pierce's pride, but late at night they'd be holding hands and talking about the old Trotskyite days. London, Hyde Park and Speakers Corner in the sixties. The fantastic anarchist hecklers. Everyone following the hecklers because they were better than the speakers.

I kept drawing the animals from Noah's Ark and I'd a copybook full of camels, giraffes, elephants, monkeys. I had started on parrots when someone saw the book. I can't remember who it was, but Pierce and Myra both wanted to be the chief discoverer.

'He's so fucking mean.' Myra pulled open the cash register trying to give me money for art materials.

'*Don't hide your bushel!*' Pierce tried to give me a wad of notes out in the barrel house. 'Don't let on to Myra, I've never met the likes of her for jealousy.'

I didn't want ordinary art classes so Myra rang up an alcoholic friend of hers who was a fantastic unconventional teacher fired years ago for her socialist principles.

'Jesus, Mary will be delighted with the few bob,' Pierce said when I was worried about disturbing her.

'She'll be a lot more delighted to be nurturing talent,' Myra said in a righteous voice.

I wouldn't let them give me any money apart from what I earned. Myra had ordered too much change from the bank and she had to pay me in fifty-pence pieces. I went to Matthews with five bags of silver. I didn't even bring Carl. I wanted to be on my own, walking through Naples Yellow, Intense Green, Mars Black. The colours of camels and deserts. What was the colour of gopher wood? What kind of a dress for Noah's wife? Lake Violet, Suede Brown, Rose. I was going to draw that four-poster bed from *The Princess and the Pea*. I reached for the biggest pad of cartridge paper.

· *Thirty-three* ·

Ger's baby turned out nice. She called it Rory and her mother took it away a lot. We were all grateful.

Ger refused to have him christened and her mother never got off her knees. Her mother was irritating, everyone called her Mrs Minahane and her beautiful face was covered in a net of lines. I imagined her in front of the mirror every night doing frowning exercises to keep up the careworn look. Her fussing over Rory was deadly, rubbing Vicks into his chest and stinking everything. There was a lot of elbowing between the two of them over the baby, but Ger said who else could she get to help?

My mother came round to my side after about six months, rang me up at Curtains and said that she wished my father would hurry up and get his heart attack so that she'd get a chance to wear all her outfits. 'I can't face the public, Maeve, with clothes gone out of fashion!'

I could have told her that half of them were back in fashion for the second time but I didn't want to startle her. I think she'd been drinking.

The week I got accepted for art school in Dublin, Ger and Tom got engaged. Myra told me that Ger was trying to upstage me. Later I overheard her fighting with Pierce, saying that Ger had her claws well into Tom now. I couldn't hear Pierce's reply.

I met Ger's mother outside the Augustinian church soon after. She was rushing in with her headscarf and a real seventies-looking missal. White leather. 'Our prayers have been answered, she's going to make that baby a Christian.'

I rang my father and he said that art schools were full of commies with no respect for land, money or government.

'Thank you for that,' I said. 'Now I'm sure that I've made the right decision.'

I ran out of money when he got to *Queer Street* but I felt half affectionate towards him as I walked away.

The christening party was at Curtains, but Jimmy Barry and Murphy weren't allowed. We all thought it was completely unfair but Pierce was adamant that they were barred. The first time he'd asserted himself since Myra found out that he was an illegitimate father.

A crowd of Teds with fierce quiffs had come down from Gurranebraher to Curtains. They had called Jimmy Barry and Murphy 'a couple of steamers' and a load of glasses had got broken. Myra had been completely useless, throwing her body across the phone box. 'You know I can't call the guards, I'm an anarchist!'

I was up until four o'clock sweeping with Pierce while Myra went off to bed with a pile of sleeping tablets.

Myra insisted that the christening party was for my leaving as well. She got an embarrassing cake enscribed 'Farewell Comrade' in the black and red colours of anarchy. Pierce told me in the barrel house that she wasn't a real anarchist at all, she only revived it to impress me.

'I'm not going to allow Maeve to be pushed out in the cold,' Myra hissed at Pierce. 'And for god's sake take an interest in that child when it comes. You are the father after all!'

'Well it will be Tom now,' Pierce said and it was so painful the way he had to pretend indifference and wait for Myra to push him over to where Tom was playing with his child.

Josie was rounded up too and she came early to make lasagne and order me around the kitchen. 'Oh to get away from Ballincollig and those stupid leaving certs. They've no more interest in French than the cat, but they all want big jobs in Brussels.' Josie kicked off her shoes and threw her emerald ring into an empty whiskey glass. Myra had to keep running into the kitchen with drinks. Claire had arrived and was playing with Rory who didn't make too much noise if you paid him enough attention.

Josie laid all the sheets of lasagne on top of each other and forgot to put the meat sauce in between. In fact she'd forgotten to *make* the meat sauce. It was such a sticky disgusting job trying to separate out the sheets of lasagne, draping them over every available plate while Josie tried to make a tomato sauce quickly. 'Forget the meat, Ger needs to lose weight anyway. It's not fair on poor old Tom the way she's let herself go. Someone asked me was she expecting again! And will I ever forget that business of the maternity dress!'

'What was that?'

'The beautiful material I bought for Ger's mother to make a maternity dress for Ger. Pure wool, any fool could see that Ger was freezing in the stuff she had. Well, Ger arrived out in this creation about six inches above her knees, no way could she wear it in her advanced state. I was absolutely scalded after all the money I'd spent. There wasn't enough material to go round, Ger said. The next thing I see is Ger's mother dashing past me into that Augustinian's church in a skirt of the same material!'

'Are you sure?'

'Am I sure after paying eleven pounds a yard? You can write it down I'm sure!'

I steered Josie back to the subject of ghosts. I was hoping that maybe I could get her to solve the mystery of our old flat with her rationality.

'Rational? Me? My grandfather? Rational? What's all this about? Didn't my grandfather nearly die of fright after he put down Aunt Lizzy's dog?'

'I knew he was wrong to put the dog down!' I exclaimed. 'If it's so bloody kind to put animals down why don't we do it to old people then!'

Josie's eyes were glazed, the wheels of invention turning inside her head. 'God, I fancy something sweet. Myra! Bring in the bottle of Baileys!'

'Well, you see, the knocking started.' Josie rapped on a roasting tin.

'I know that bit. It was just the wind knocking the handle of the blind against the window. And that poor dog crying.'

'Ah that was the *first* time, were you listening at all? You're so dreamy Maeve! Well if you were listening you'd have heard me telling how the knocking and howling started again *after* the dog was shot.'

'Oh god!'

'Oh yes! It nearly drove my grandfather off his head. All those girls had very bad hearts you know.'

'Did he bring them downstairs again to investigate?'

'With their bad hearts? And nothing below in that

room, only a gale-force wind? Of course he did not! Six times he got a carpenter in to fix the latch in the end. The man refused to come any more, he said that it was giving him desperate nightmares.'

'So how did they stop it?'

'They didn't, it just went on night after night, knock, knock, knock. Howl, howl, howl.' Josie pounded on the roasting tin and threw her head back to shake the hair out of her eyes. 'Serves him right, the old tyrant!'

'Who?'

'My grandfather of course, sure Aunt Lizzy wasn't from the servant class! She only went to America to get away from him!' Josie banged the roasting tin again.

Carl stuck his head in the door, looking worried, but I beckoned him away.

'So then what happened?'

'Nothing.'

'Nothing?'

'They had to move out, build a new house. My grandfather got pneumonia in the move.'

'So that was the end of him?'

'Not at all, he recovered. Didn't he drive me mad with his old stick and his rosary beads when I was a child.'

'So the house must be still haunted?' I asked, wondering if it was the grandfather who was doing the haunting. He seemed very supernatural to me. The way his health waxed and waned. The way he seemed to keep rising up with a different personality. Really deadly. Like God in the Old Testament.

'Although the farm has been sold and the house rebuilt many times, people still hear the dog. Sometimes howling. Sometimes whimpering. Children seem to like it. It's the parents who take leave of their

senses.' Josie's eyes had begun to roll in her head. I'd
have to call Tom. And Tom would have to lay down
the law about her drinking again.

He blamed her grandfather for the unhappy child-
hood that she couldn't forget. The pendulum never
stopped swinging. She loved him, she hated him. She
wanted to kill him even though he was dead. Tom said
that it was no wonder Josie was an alcoholic with a
grandfather like that poisoning the generations.

He did sound like that rat. PASSPORT! PASSPORT!
YOU HAVEN'T PAID YOUR TOLL!

I'd worked something else out for myself through
observing Murphy. If you blamed your parents for the
bad things then you had to be consistent and praise
them for the happiness in your life.

Murphy told everyone he met that his mother was
an alcoholic and beat the legs off him every day of his
life until he got strong enough to hold her hands. But
Murphy could also tell stories about his mother singing
him to sleep, massaging his bruised legs, fumes of
cheap wine wreathing round his head. He'd break
your heart.

Jimmy Barry was saving up for a steel plate for his
father's dog's hip. He nearly broke his other hand,
punching the wall with embarrassment when we found
out about it.

Strong bonds were full of love and hate. Power
sharing wasn't just hard for politicians. *You're wresting
for power,* my father told me and I owed it to him not
to let him oppress me. If he was going to haunt me I
was going to let it happen openly. I didn't want it
creeping out in glasses of wine or oudja boards. Afraid
of a creaking floorboard, the whistle of the wind in
my own breath.

If I didn't blow the whole thing open, who is to say

one of my children mightn't be dangling off a bar stool in years to come heading for Queer Street? She might anyway, but at least I'd tried to break the chain.

Claire told me that X-rays weren't black and white the way people thought they were. X-rays were grey. Doctors read the different shades. Subjective. In spite of all his talk about bourgeois pigs, Pierce had barred Jimmy Barry and Murphy because of where they came from. I found out from Myra that Best had broken all the front windows in seventy-nine and was still allowed back.

People thought that fairy tales were black and white. They weren't. They were grey. I read the different shades. Where fairy tales met anarchy and bullies got their comeuppance. Murphy was an ugly duckling. Like Hans Christian Anderson. Subversive. Painting the emperor with no clothes on.